WANDER NO MORE

Books by Paul Stutzman

The Wandering Home Series
Book One: The Wanderers
Book Two: Wandering Home
Book Three: Wander No More

Adventure Memoir
Hiking Through
     One Man's Journey to Peace and Freedom on the
     Appalachian Trail
Biking Across America
     My Coast-to-Coast Adventure and the People I Met Along
     the Way
Stuck in the Weeds
     A Pilgrim on the Mississippi River and the Camino de
     Santiago

With Author Serena Miller
More Than Happy: The Wisdom of Amish Parenting

Contact
www.paulstutzman.com
www.facebook.com/pvstutzman
pstutzman@roadrunner.com

Wander No More

Paul Stutzman

Wandering Home Books
Berlin, Ohio

But the path of the just is as the shining light,
that shineth more and more unto the perfect day.
Proverbs 4:18

಑ಒ

PROLOGUE

October 2017

Johnny grinned as he recalled a conversation he had overheard between his father and mother years earlier. He was now busy hitching the horse to the buggy, but he had done this so often that his fingers worked confidently and had no need of directives from his brain. His thoughts were busy, instead, recalling what he had heard as a young child.

"I am sure that some marriages would be better off," Mandy had declared emphatically.

John had smiled at the fervor in his wife's voice. "Or maybe worse off," he had said, with a teasing tone.

"John!" she had fired back in mock reproach, and they had both laughed.

Back then, all the secondary roads in the Milford community were gravel. Buggy wheels were constructed of wood, and most had a steel band encircling the wheel to support and preserve the form. As a buggy traveled down the country byways, steel met gravel, and the resulting clatter made conversations almost impossible—unless conducted at shouting level. A paved road was a welcome sight.

Some Amish churches were beginning to allow their members to use wheels with a rubber band instead of the metal one. This deadened the sound considerably and made normal conversation possible. One of the groups permitting such modernity was the New Order Amish, a branch that had broken away from the Old Order Amish Church.

Johnny's father was a bishop in the Old Order church, and when the bishops of neighboring areas met occasionally to discuss rules and regulations, John would sometimes bring up the possibility of allowing buggy-wheel "silencers." It was a practical consideration, and consensus seemed to be moving that way. However, one old, rigid traditionalist would not budge.

"It's how we've always done it," he would say. "It was good enough for our elders, and allowing this will just lead to giving in to other desires." It was the same answer he gave to discussions on many other widely diverse issues.

How times have changed, Dad, thought Johnny, suddenly wishing for a conversation with his dad, accompanied by a piece of Mandy's pie and her strong black coffee.

The Amish community here was thriving and growing, and, just as John had foreseen, not only was good farmland becoming scarce and expensive for young men starting out, but agricultural land was also being eaten up by housing developments, factories, and tourist businesses. The Amish were working at other jobs, many of which were in the construction business, which was booming. Enterprising men had started their own carpenter and masonry crews and were becoming known for their fair prices and quality work. And as the tourism phenomenon had hit the area and outsiders discovered the peace and tranquility of Amish Country, cottage industries had sprung up all over the area: furniture shops, cheese shops, quilt shops, lodging establishments, and a myriad of other businesses that provided employment for Amish workers and catered to millions of visitors.

In their daily life, the Amish were on the move more than they had ever been before. Communication was essential, both with the outside world and within their own community. Leadership made decisions, one of which was that cell phones could be used to conduct business. Then the cat jumped out of the bag rather quickly. In no time, some Amish folks were using cell phones at will.

What wasn't considered at the time—by both the English and the Amish—was that the convenience and astonishing capabilities of the modern phone would also provide a camera, videos, and the Internet. The world suddenly overwhelmed unsuspecting users of cell phones, regardless of their church affiliation or whether or not their house had electricity.

Noisy buggy wheels no longer mattered much; Strawberry Lane and virtually all dirt roads were now paved. Instead, Amish bishops had to deal with other, much more insidious evils—all those things English people also faced in the world.

Three of Johnny's grandchildren, who were visiting with him, came running from his sister's big house at the foot of Strawberry Hill.

"Grandpa, are we taking a buggy ride? Will you take us up to see the big cross?"

"Sure, kids, hop in. Can everyone get in there?" he asked as the three little ones tried to scramble up into the buggy. He gave each a helpful boost, then climbed in himself, gingerly trying to find room between the wiggling young bodies.

Johnny placed the reins in the hands of one grandson and told him to give the leather straps a quick slap on the horse's hindquarters.

"Yell *giddy up* real loud," he instructed.

The child did, and the horse took off with a start, much to the enjoyment of the buggy's occupants. Soon laughter and shouts of joy drifted down the hill and over the valley as the buggy moved up Strawberry Hill toward an enormous cross erected at the crest.

Atop the hill, Johnny pulled the horse into a field lane adjacent to a small cemetery. He tied the horse to a tree, and the children all disembarked. Pausing for just a moment, Johnny gazed across Strawberry Lane at the towering cross. Then his attention came back to the cemetery. He swung open the gate in the white fence and led the little parade inside, pointing out several stone markers.

"Remember Annie, the lady I've told you about? It's because of her that the cross was built here, and," his loving glance took in all of them, "it's also why *you* all exist."

He squatted down.

"These two graves beside Annie are your great grandparents, John and Mandy." How Mandy would have loved to see these great-grandchildren running around the farm. "As you see, there are a few spaces yet beside Annie."

"But, Grandpa, how did that lady Annie build that cross if she's dead?" inquired the oldest, Johnny's only granddaughter.

"Let's go over there, and I'll explain," said Johnny, standing up and taking the hand of the youngest child.

It was still early and no tourists had yet been compelled to make the trek to the cross. One vehicle was parked nearby, but no visitor could be seen.

Johnny stood for a moment, his head tilted back, gazing up at the white cross outlined against a cloudless blue sky.

"I'll tell you a story, children," he began. "You see, I was married to Annie. She got hurt, and went to Heaven, and I was very confused and sad. So I took a bicycle ride from California to Texas. One day in Texas, I saw a cross much like this in the distance and it drew me to it. That day at the cross, I found out how much God loved me.

"It changed my life. I began to see all the ways that God was guiding my life and providing for me. And my life took a different turn …"

He abandoned his narrative as memories came back and pushed aside the present reality.

The children waited a few seconds for him to go on, then, seeing that he was not going to do so immediately, they left him and started a game of tag, running around the base of the cross and hopping up and down the steps where words were engraved in the stone.

"The cross changed everything," Johnny said quietly, as his thoughts sifted through the events of another time.

1

Who might be next? The question was often whispered in the Amish community following the close deaths of two people. *Bad things happen in threes,* they often said.

"But this time," Johnny Miller muttered to himself as he opened the screen door, "all three came within seconds of each other."

The rattle of the screen door closing behind him echoed through the house. Too empty. *You'd think I'd be used to this by now. But I'm not.*

He slid his hat onto the shelf above the coat hooks and dropped his bag on the floor by the kitchen table, where his sister had left a neat stack of mail. Without picking up the long white envelope on top of the pile, Johnny knew it was another check from Sydney. The money just kept coming, and Johnny wasn't quite sure what to do with it or even how to consider this stream of income. There was also a catalog from a company selling nutrition supplements for horses. He'd been waiting impatiently for this information, but now, he realized, it didn't matter at all.

At the bottom of the pile was the thick weekly newspaper, *The Budget.* The harsh black headlines stabbed at his mind and heart, already numb from days of shock. His chest felt tight as he picked up the paper, sank into the chair where Annie had spent her last night, and began to read:

THREE DEAD IN CAR/BUGGY CRASH
Henry and Betty Graber of Harrison Mills, Indiana, and their young daughter Esther died in a car-buggy crash on County Road 55 early Friday afternoon.

Johnny had no need to read every word. He'd already heard the details too many times. The buggy had been hit broadside. The car, traveling at a high rate of speed, had not paused or even slowed at the stop sign. The driver was the mayor of the next town over, and he had tried to claim he was blinded by the afternoon sun and never noticed the stop sign. But everyone knew the sun was still high in the sky when the three died, and every local knew that stop sign had been there for decades. The mayor had been drunk, the gossip claimed. Drunk, at one o'clock in the afternoon.

Johnny laid the paper aside and rested his head on the back of the chair, closing his eyes.

The funeral had brought back so many emotions, as sharp as though Annie's funeral had been only yesterday. But Henry and Betty had died together; neither had left the other to go on alone, as he had been left alone when Annie died.

Instead, the Grabers had left behind their older daughter, Christine.

He had been amazed at how much Christine had grown. She was six years old now and in school. That was the reason she had not been in the buggy with her family. Now she was a little girl without a mommy or daddy or little sister. While Christine had laughed and run at recess with her friends and then bent over her desk, learning to read and write, her world had crumbled and disappeared.

What would happen to her? Of course, in the Amish community, family always stepped in to care for children. But Johnny could not erase the picture of her bewildered little face. The petite features and dark hair and blue eyes were Annie, 20 years ago. Johnny had no way of sorting out whether the ache he felt was only for Christine's sadness or for his own loss, when her mother had left him and this house to move on to another life in Heaven.

His parents and sister would expect him at the big house for supper. It was a rare thing for him to turn down a meal at his mother's table, but Johnny would really rather have stayed home, here in the quiet of his and Annie's house. He wanted to read her journals again, especially the letter she had written to him just before she died. He wanted time alone to think about those few brief moments when he had seen her at the gates of Heaven, and he wanted to go back and try to remember her words to him about Christine.

But they would be expecting him. His family would want to hear about the funeral and any other news of acquaintances. No one else had gone to Indiana for the funeral. Naomi's wedding was less than two weeks away, and spring planting was still not finished. But Johnny was, after all, a brother-in-law to Betty and Henry. He had been the one to go.

He stood up reluctantly. He would have to go for supper. And of course there would be no way to avoid talking about Annie. In the last two years, he had often found comfort in reminiscing with his family about his wife—they had all loved her so—but tonight he would have preferred to be alone with his memories.

***

The world was expected to go on as normal the next day. Johnny was happy to be back at the milking and morning chores.

In some ways, the routine provided a daily structure that gave him comfort and helped him stay grounded. At the same time, though, he also used routine as a refuge where he could hide from outside forces and pretend all was well.

Supper the night before had been, as he expected, a somber affair, heavy with sadness. This morning, though, even while every one of the Miller household still held thoughts of Annie's family at the edges of their minds, the daily business of farm and wedding bubbled up and charged the conversation at the breakfast table.

"Mom, it doesn't look like the lilacs are going to be blooming in time," Naomi said, standing on tiptoe and peering out the window over the sink. "What are we going to use for the bridal table?"

"We have almost two weeks yet." Mandy was trying to be reassuring. "And Martha's bushes have more southern exposure, so we'll check on hers. I'm going over there today to talk with her about last-minute details on the meal. John, are you going to send someone else to pick up the chicken, or should I plan to go myself?"

John looked up from his bacon and eggs with a look on his face that said he had not yet thought about fetching the chicken to be cooked for the wedding meal. But while he was considering his answer, Naomi went on to the next item that needed attention.

"I guess I'll have to walk down to the phone booth and call the store again today. Those special serving dishes that were back-ordered have still not come in. I should have ordered them much sooner, but I just hadn't thought of it before, and then when I saw the samples … "

Johnny wasn't listening to most of the women's talk. He was thinking about what had to be done in the barn before he could get into the fields that morning. He'd been away from the soil for almost a week; it was time to be tending his farm again.

They finished their meal as usual, with John's reading of Scripture and prayer. Then Naomi and her mother were up and clearing the table, hurrying into their day as they whisked the dishes through the dishwater. Johnny pushed back his chair and rose, his mind already in the barn.

"Son, hold on a minute," said John. He picked up an envelope that had been lying beside his breakfast plate. Johnny had noticed it there but had felt no curiosity. His father regarded the envelope for a minute, seeming to debate something with himself. Then he withdrew a single sheet of paper covered on both sides with large handwriting.

"I received this letter yesterday from Bishop Orin Borntrager, out in the Nappanee area. Seems like a young man in his church district met an untimely end in a farming accident."

Johnny knew instantly what request the letter contained.

"He was only married for three years and left two small children. The bishop is inquiring about the possibility of arranging a visit between the two of you."

This was common when tragedy struck. Amish communities, even though separated by hundreds of miles, often attempted to put families back together—or, at least, to put their people back into whole families once again, even though the original family could never be rebuilt.

This wasn't the first time Johnny had been approached about meeting a young widow. Thus far, he had always politely declined.

"Dad—" he began now, with a slow shake of his head. *Just let me get to work.*

"Audrey will have a car. And she said she wants to help with whatever still has to be done. Maybe she could go," Naomi was saying to her mother.

The name rose above the noise of running water, silverware clinking in the sink, and his father's words.

Johnny's mind had been halfway to the barn. Now it hustled back into the house as he strained to hear the women's conversation.

His father's voice interfered. "The two children are a girl and a boy, one and two years old."

"Her last letter mentioned how excited she was to see—"

Oh! Naomi had turned away just as she finished that sentence, and Johnny could not catch the ending.

Did she say she was excited to see all of us? Or did she mention me?

"They farm a lot of corn out there in Nappanee," his dad was saying.

"I'm so glad she'll be here early. We'll have some time to talk." Naomi was talking faster than usual, and Johnny could hear the excitement in her voice.

When? When was she arriving? He had known Audrey would be at the wedding, but he had somehow missed that she would be coming early. And she was staying here!

"They would, of course, keep your visit confidential, should you be interested in meeting with Elisabeth."

Elisabeth? Her name is Audrey.

"Johnny? Are you listening?"

"Yes, Dad … "

Audrey … in a cornfield …

***

Johnny walked to the barn with his thoughts in total chaos. His refuge had been breached. His safe, structured routine had been shattered for that morning.

The face of Annie's daughter still lingered at the edges of his brain. Or was it Annie's face? He had not yet had a chance to go back to his wife's letter. Then Elisabeth and cornfields hundreds of miles away stood waiting for an answer. He brushed that image away. But the most disturbing intruder was a secret, something he had dared not even admit to himself. And that secret was beginning to push itself out into his consciousness, demanding a hearing.

2

Johnny's safe routine, it turned out, had been disrupted not only for that morning but for days. It had been two days since he first heard Audrey's name mentioned at breakfast, and somehow that had cracked and splintered all his focus as he tried to prepare the barn and farm for the big event, Naomi's wedding.

He found it curious that even when he was sweeping the barn and moving hay and machinery, his thoughts went to a day in California. Yes, he *had* reminisced briefly about the time two years ago when they had gone through the same preparations for his own wedding to Annie. But those faded memories were pushed aside by thoughts of the guests who would soon sit here to witness Paul and Naomi's marriage. Thoughts of *one* guest, to be more exact.

It had been a year since any of the Millers had seen Audrey. Naomi had kept in touch with her, writing and receiving letters weekly. In addition, Audrey had sent newsletters from the orphanage in Mexico where she was now teaching. The newsletters had been addressed to the entire Miller family, so Johnny had read about Audrey's work in the orphanage that her mother had built. He did not always read the entire pamphlet, but he had always scanned the photos, looking for the face he remembered, even though he would not acknowledge the irrepressible feelings of both satisfaction and excitement that went through him when he did see her image captured by the camera, always with children around her and always with that smile that had first dazzled him.

He thought he had put the whole matter and all those feelings to rest when he had thrown away Audrey's letter, the day after he left her family's house in Malibu. He had cut his ties to her—whatever ties might have been spun in the one afternoon they had spent together. For a few hours as he pedaled along the California coast, he had allowed himself to imagine …. and then he had realized the impossibility of it all and he had slammed shut the door, refusing to open it even a crack. He was a farmer. She was a California city girl. He was Amish. She was not.

Still, he always checked the pictures in the newsletter.

He also had no idea what Audrey now thought about him—or if she thought of him at all. Of course, she probably did; he was Naomi's brother, and she and Naomi had become close friends. But the last month that Audrey and Johnny had spent together, he had treated her as a stranger.

She *was* a stranger to him then. His violent collision with a truck had blocked all memory of her, of the afternoon they had spent together in the mountains of California, and of the big red horse that had almost brought them together. During his time in the hospital, he had understood Audrey's presence as a friend of Naomi and as someone who helped his family while he lay immovable and broken. But his mind could never quite put the pieces of the puzzle together and figure out *how* Audrey knew his family, but she was there. She had meant nothing to him then, because he could remember nothing of their story.

Until the day when the amnesia finally lifted and he remembered everything. But by then, he had walked away from the hospital and Audrey and the life that had been offered to him in California. And by then, he had no idea what to say to her.

And so he had not spoken or written to Audrey since.

She had never quite left his mind, though. It was as though she occupied a corner room way back at the edge of his consciousness, behind a door that he kept tightly shut. She was always there, but on the door was a forbidding sign: DO NOT ENTER.

There were times that he walked by and glanced at that door, like the times he browsed through the orphanage newsletter looking for her picture. But he felt slightly guilty about even that small action. And he knew he could never, ever touch the doorknob.

***

"Where's Dad?" Naomi's voice interrupted his swirling thoughts. He threw the forkful of straw and manure onto the spreader and looked at his sister.

"Down at the sawmill."

"Mom and I are going back up to Martha's. We won't be gone long. Back for supper."

"Okay."

Naomi stood looking at her brother as he kept on cleaning the stall.

"What's going on with you? You haven't been yourself since you got back from the funeral."

He didn't answer, but threw another forkful.

Her mouth curved into a slight smile and her eyebrows wiggled upward.

"Ohhh ...You're thinking about Audrey coming today, aren't you?"

He tried to dance away from answering her directly. Unfortunately, his sister knew him too well.

"What time do you expect her?" he asked, instead of answering her question. He kept working and did not look at Naomi.

"Not till late tonight."

Good. He would be in his own house, in bed. He would have to face her eventually. But at least not tonight. Tomorrow, maybe. He could not avoid her. But maybe the women would keep her busy with errands and odd jobs as they prepared for the wedding.

"Johnny …" Naomi paused and watched him work. Then she turned away.

"We'll be back in time to have supper on the table."

It seemed she had decided not to say what was on her mind. That was a bit unlike her, but Johnny was relieved. He did not want to talk to her about Audrey.

How could he? He didn't even know what he *thought* about Audrey. He'd kept the door to that room closed too tightly, always obeying the DO NOT ENTER sign.

***

The cows had dutifully filed into their stanchions, proceeded with devouring their feed, and stood patiently as Johnny and his father drained their heavy bags of the warm milk. Johnny carried a full pail into the milk house and poured it through the strainer into the milk can.

It had been a long day. He had worked at twice the speed as usual, as though his frenzied pace would shake off the thoughts that buzzed around inside his head and would not leave him in peace. His clothes showed the stains of the day's work. He would be happy to get to the house, clean up, and sit down to read the paper. Then a good night's rest. And tomorrow, he would face whatever he had to face.

He came back out of the milk house.

And there she stood, talking to John.

Tall, *elegant*—that was the word that came to his mind—in a simple, natural way. Her auburn hair was pulled back in the same ponytail he remembered. And the green eyes that turned to him were just as intense as he remembered. It was impossible to miss the light that flared up in those eyes when she caught sight of him.

"Johnny?" It was almost a question. Of course, he now looked like an Amish man, not the English man she had met a year ago.

"Audrey!"

They stood, looking at each other. Then he realized she was smiling a delighted smile.

"Hi," she said, mischief in her eyes. "You look a little different than the last time I saw you."

"I hope so," he replied.

Still smiling, she turned back to John, only to find that he had sat down beside one of the cows and started to milk again. She turned back to Johnny.

"Sorry to surprise you. But no one was at the house, so I thought I'd look around."

"Naomi's at her sister's. She's not expecting you until late tonight."

Johnny could think only of how he must look to her—and how he smelled. And here she was, standing in their barn, looking so serene and lovely and perfect and … clean.

"I know. But I had a chance to take an earlier flight. And I couldn't call to let you know." She looked around, with the smile still on her face. "Well, I guess I won't be much use here. I don't want to get in your way, so I'll just go to the house and wait."

***

The wide, delighted smile was still on Audrey's face as they sat down for supper. The meal was a bit late; when Naomi had arrived home and found her friend waiting, there had been a time of hugs and excited chatter, and supper preparations had been delayed. Then Audrey had joined Mandy and Naomi in the kitchen, and a quick meal soon appeared on the table.

Johnny had had a chance to change his clothes and take a shower. He had looked at himself in the mirror. His beard had grown longer, and the black suspenders over his gray shirt and his bowl haircut all labeled him an Amish man. But for the first time in over a year, the question rose up. *Is this what you really are?*

He was instantly angry with himself. He had made his choice. He had returned to the farm. He *was* a farmer. This was his life. The decision was made, and temptation to think about other choices and other possibilities would only bring him restlessness and discontent. He must squash such thoughts.

He felt more composed as he walked back to the big house to join the rest of the family and Audrey for supper. Naomi's soon-to-be husband, Paul, was there, too. Johnny was grateful for his friend's presence. He was one more person at the table to keep the talk going.

Tonight, Johnny planned to be a spectator, not a part of the conversation. His thoughts were so scattered that he was almost afraid to open his mouth. He wanted to wait, quietly, until he regained his balance. Of course, this was quite out of character for him, and he knew his changed demeanor was obvious to his family. He did not miss the glances that his mother and sister threw his way.

They had been talking about the orphanage when he first walked into the kitchen.

"I feel as though I've found the spot in this world where I belong," Audrey was saying. "Those years in college, in books and lectures, seemed so dry and uninspiring, there were times I wanted to give it up and just get to work. Now I'm glad I lasted. It's all worth it. I've only been in Mexico one year, and already I feel as if I've made a difference in those little lives. They need someone to love them. They've become like family, almost like my own children."

"But your mother isn't there full time, is she?" asked Mandy.

"No. As a matter of fact, she's rarely there. Her talents lie in fund-raising and administration. She loves that. She's already busy building the next orphanage, this time in Columbia. We have a native director who lives next door to the orphanage. I'm sure you've seen his notes in the newsletter. He and his wife have five children of their own, but it's as though they've adopted this entire family of sixteen more children."

"But ... I mean ... you're there *alone?"* persisted Mandy.

Audrey looked thoughtful.

"No, Mandy, I'm really not alone. I have my adopted family. And Jesus. That makes all the difference for me. No, no. I'm not there alone."

Johnny remembered his conversation with Audrey that day, a year before, as they drove through the mountains to the Cohraine horse farm. Audrey's small family had all been going separate ways, even then. Her mother traveled a great deal, her father was a busy, successful divorce attorney with Hollywood clients, and her sister was studying art in Italy. To his mind, there was already a great deal of *aloneness* in their lives even before Audrey had moved to Mexico.

"Do you teach in Spanish or English?" asked Paul.

"Spanish, mostly. But we see the value of children also knowing English, and they pick it up quickly, so there are times when English slips into our conversations, too." She looked as if a new thought had just occurred to her. "Actually, I'm the only person there whose first language is English."

"I just can't believe that people would abandon their babies," said Naomi.

"It is hard to understand, but it's a very poor area, and sometimes parents know that their little ones will get better care—

food and clothes—at the orphanage than at home. Or sometimes the children need medical care that the parents just can't afford. So some of our children aren't really orphans in the strict sense of the word."

"Did you get my last letter?" asked Naomi. "The one about Annie's daughter, Christine?"

"Yes. That was such sad news. What will happen to that little girl? Do Amish send children to orphanages? Or perhaps here in the States they would be placed in foster homes?"

"No," John said. "Usually relatives will step in and take the children into their families and raise them as their own. She will be cared for, I'm sure of it."

Johnny saw the tears in Audrey's eyes, and he felt his own smarting. He blinked quickly, but Audrey's tears spilled over and laid two wet streaks down each cheek. She seemed to take no notice.

"But that little girl lost her whole family. It breaks my heart to see little children in such sad and painful situations."

"Well, dear," said Mandy, "I think you are indeed in the right spot on this earth."

***

He came home to his own small, quiet house and settled into Annie's chair with a great sense of relief. The evening had gone smoothly enough, and he had never been forced to have a conversation alone with Audrey.

She was everything he remembered—he had never really forgotten her at all, except for those weeks of amnesia resulting from the accident and the coma. Audrey was lovely, smart, and down-to-earth, and she soon made people feel comfortable with her. She had gained something, though, since he had met her in California. Purpose? Contentment? Passion? Vision? What was it?

He couldn't put a name to it, but Audrey had found something that seemed to be guiding her life and giving her strength and energy.

He sighed and decided he didn't want to think about her anymore that night.

Reaching over to the little table by the chair, he lifted Annie's journal. Flipping to the last page with writing, he again read the unfinished line—the very last words his wife had written to him: *Oh, Johnny, one last thing, Christine will need*

The words trailed off into unreadable squiggles. Annie had lost consciousness at that point and died a few hours later.

What would Christine need? Could Annie have possibly known or had a glimpse of what was going to happen? How was that possible?

He closed his eyes and again recalled the last time he had seen his wife. He had been in a bicycle accident, hit by a truck as he pedaled a road in Texas. He had died, according to the doctors. But he had felt alive. And then he had seen Annie again, even though she had left the earth seven months before. She had met him at the gates of Heaven.

There she had repeated the words about Christine. He had been ready to enter Heaven with Annie, when she had told him he had to go back. He had wanted to stay with her and tried to refuse to leave, but Annie said, "Yes, dear, you will go back. Christine is going to need you."

And then Annie had disappeared, Heaven had slipped away, and he was back in a hospital in Texas, in agony—both physical and emotional.

That had been a year ago, just after he had made the decision to come home and remain in the Amish church. He had come home to the valley and the farm and tried to settle back into life the way it had always been. But he had found that, other than the seasons and the soil and the crops, nothing was the way it had always been.

And now, even this world that he had trusted to be his solid and unchanging fortress had been shaken. Because now the door to that corner room stood open, the sign had fluttered away, and Audrey was here.

3

Audrey's first thought was, *Here I am, right here in the middle of a world I've only dreamed about.*

A rooster crowed as the early morning light slipped past the edges of the plain blue curtain and began transforming the bedroom. A dog barked twice. *It sounds like home,* was her second thought. At home, the sun's rays would be slipping past the dark purple of the mountain as the village came alive. By habit, her thoughts went to preparation for the day's classes. Then they shifted to the present. *No, I'm here. In Ohio. On Johnny's farm. In Naomi's house.*

She pulled the quilt closer around her neck and smiled.

Naomi had often written about the Miller family's life on the farm. And Naomi had such a vivid way of writing that Audrey felt that she had been to this place before and she had been a part of this life. Or that the farm life had become a part of her. Now she was actually here.

Naomi's letters had held little about Johnny, though. He had made his choice, it seemed, to return to the Amish church and lifestyle. When Audrey had first met him, he was a widower on a quest to find a new life. The spark that had ignited between them was obvious to everyone, including Samuel Cohraine, Audrey's father. She had been embarrassed at the exorbitant offer of employment that Samuel had made to Johnny. An astonishing salary. A truck. Lodging at their home, in the guest house. A share in the horse-race winnings and later stud fees. *Oh, and marry my daughter. I noticed you two seemed to like each other.* Samuel had never said that, of course, but to Audrey's ears, it seemed as though she were part of the package offered to Johnny, if only he would stay in California and help Samuel train his race horses.

But Johnny had made his choice and kept moving on in his search for a new life.

Then the call had come to Samuel's law office; Johnny, pedaling along on a bicycle, had been hit by a truck. He had died, actually, but the doctors were able to revive him. Within two hours of the phone call, Samuel and Audrey were on a plane, headed to the hospital in Texas.

Johnny had lain for days, unconscious, in the hazy land between life and death. The Millers had come, too, several days later. That's when Audrey had first met Johnny's family. And over the ensuing weeks, as they waited for Johnny to recuperate, Audrey and Naomi had become close friends. *Like sisters*, Naomi would sometimes write. Except that almost every aspect of their outward lives was vastly different.

Audrey heard a door open and close, and soft footsteps padded to her door, paused a moment outside, and then went on down the hall. That would be Naomi, wondering if she were awake. She suddenly threw off the quilt and rolled out of bed. She didn't want to be a pampered guest. She wanted to be a part of this life that she had for so long tried to imagine.

***

He had expected it. But still, the sight was something of a shock.

Johnny came into the kitchen for breakfast, and there, frying eggs at his mother's stove, was Audrey. Her back was turned to him, but she turned as Johnny and his father came into the room.

"Good morning, gentlemen," she said with a smile that lit her entire face.

Through morning devotions and prayer and the breakfast conversation about the day's work, Johnny found it hard to focus his thoughts. Audrey, in the Millers' kitchen. He had never expected to see this, and the ease with which she seemed to settle into their morning routine—and even become a part of it—took him by surprise.

"I have the rental car. I can run errands," Audrey was saying.

"That will certainly help," Mandy said.

"Please, put me to work. Whatever needs to be done. Cleaning, cooking, lawn work, I can even muck stalls—I'm not sure about milking, though. I've never tried that."

Johnny gave his attention to carefully buttering a biscuit, but he couldn't resist saying, "Are you sure you know what you're offering?"

His biscuit needed a bit of honey, too, which he swirled carefully, but he could *feel* Audrey smiling at him.

"Probably not. But I want to be of use," she said firmly. "And I want to be part of … of this."

***

So they put her to work, and she was happy to be busy. Mandy had food to fix and windows to be washed. One day Audrey cooked a Mexican lunch for the family. She went to Stevenson when John asked her to pick up a packet of papers from the title office. (She guessed that he couldn't quite bring himself to ask a lady guest to clean out a stall or do other barn chores.) The next day, she was on the road to Stevenson again; the extra china that

Naomi had ordered had finally come in and Naomi wanted to pick it up immediately.

"I love it here," Audrey told Naomi as they drove to Stevenson. "You've described your life so well in your letters over the last year that I thought I could imagine what life was like on an Amish farm. But it's not at all what I expected."

Naomi laughed and looked closely at her friend.

"What did you expect?"

"Well, already the reality has pushed away some of my expectations, and I can't even remember what I imagined … but I can tell you about things that have surprised me. For one thing, I didn't understand how interconnected your lives are with your extended family and your neighbors. My family is scattered for much of the year, and I barely know many of our neighbors in Malibu. Although, in our little village in Mexico, I do feel more like part of the community.

"And then, the peace, for another thing. I always sensed that you were so contented with your life, but I did not grasp how peaceful your valley is. It's a balm for the soul."

"Oh, but our lives are not always that way. We have sorrows and grief, just like you do. We've seen disasters. We have to deal with all the same things the English do. We all live in the same world, after all."

"But somehow, this part of the country—it's like nothing I ever knew in California, and certainly not like my little spot in Mexico."

"No, I suppose not." Naomi was quiet for a moment. "I've never really seen much of the world outside our community. That trip last year to Corpus Christi was the most I've ever been away from here. It was quite enough city and big world for me. I was so glad to be home again. But that time I spent there with Johnny in the hospital did show me that here we live in a … well, I would say a protected world."

"You did really well in the big city—for a country girl."

Both of them laughed.

"Audrey, I know I've said it often, but we were—I was—so grateful to have you there to help me. I would have been lost without you. Afraid to step out of the hospital, even."

"You know I wanted to be there," replied Audrey, sobering. "What do you think, Naomi? What's Johnny thinking? I noticed he's the only one of your family who hasn't sent me on errands or asked for help with anything. He seems to be avoiding me as much as he can. He won't even look me in the eye when we're having a meal. I've prayed about this. I didn't know what it would be like, coming here. I mean, of course I wanted to be here for your big day, I wanted to meet Paul, and see all your family again, but … I just don't know what to do with Johnny."

Naomi raised her eyebrows at her friend, "*Do* with Johnny?"

Audrey felt the warmth creep up her neck. She kept her eyes on the road, but smiled as she shook her head.

"Silly. You know what I mean. I don't know how to treat him. How he wants to be treated. The Johnny I met in California was a different man. Then, after his accident, he had no memory of me, and after he did regain his memory, he never wrote or contacted me again. I thought … I thought we had a special connection. I know he made his choice to come back here, farm, and remain Amish, but still … I thought …"

Feeling slightly foolish, she gave a slight shrug of her shoulders and glanced at Naomi and was startled to see tears in her friend's eyes.

"I will tell you something," Naomi began. "Growing up, my brother and I were best friends. When it seemed he was leaving the Amish, at first I thought it just could not happen. We would be going two separate pathways in life. That thought hurt for a while. Then I started praying for God's best in Johnny's life. And once I believed that God did have a hand in whatever Johnny did, then I was at peace with whatever came. Even though part of me still hurt.

"That was all during the time Johnny was on his bike ride and we knew so little about where he was or what he was doing or thinking. Then came his accident, and I wondered how God could possibly be working through that. And then I met you ..."

Audrey realized she was holding her breath, waiting for Naomi to go on. She let herself slowly exhale.

"Then I met you, and I believed that God had brought a woman into Johnny's life that would be the best for him. I came home from the hospital in Texas believing that you were going to be my sister-in-law. I believed you were the miracle for Johnny that I had been praying for."

Audrey gave a small, quiet sound. There were tears in her eyes now, too.

"It didn't quite turn out that way, did it?" she said.

"No, I guess not. Johnny made his decision. He was so happy to be back home. I know he loves farming, and we were happy to have him home. The church welcomed him back."

"Does he love the church, Naomi?"

Audrey heard her own words spoken before she had a chance to think about them.

"Oh, I'm sorry. That was the wrong question. I just meant—"

"It's all right," Naomi said quickly. "I understand what you're wondering. Well, he made the choice. And being a part of the Amish church is different than it is for an English person who might belong to a church. Every part of our life is affected by our connection to the church. If a person chooses to leave the Amish, that usually means he is leaving almost everything about his life. He often moves away, he loses his community, he might find a new job and a new circle of friends, and sometimes, he even loses his family, in a sense. Leaving the Amish church really is leaving one life behind and going on to another one."

"I can see that, just in the few days I've been here," Audrey said. "So in coming back here, Johnny chose a life, not just a church."

"Yes."

Both were quiet.

Audrey took a deep breath.

"And do you think he'll marry again? Is that part of choosing this life?"

Naomi smiled at her, though Audrey kept her eyes on the road.

"I suppose. If he chooses to. I would guess that not many young men want to stay unmarried. And in our churches, young widows and widowers are often matched up, but so far, Johnny hasn't seemed interested."

Audrey weighed this information.

"So, back to my original question. What's he thinking? How do I *treat* him? How do I talk to him?"

Naomi was quiet for so long that Audrey feared she had blundered again with her question. Still, she and Naomi had always been frank with each other, and the differences between *Amish* and *English* had never seemed to hinder their friendship.

Naomi finally spoke.

"You're right. He has been acting a bit uncomfortable and awkward since you're here. Well, it actually started before you were here—I saw the change in him the day he realized you were coming to the wedding. I think …"

Naomi paused. Audrey waited, hearing that her friend was searching for the right words.

"Johnny has a lot going on in his head right now, with Annie's daughter suddenly losing her family, and a preacher in Indiana wanting to arrange a meeting between Johnny and a widow out there." Audrey's heart sank at the mention of this, only to be lifted up again when Naomi went on quickly, "But I don't see much chance of that happening. He hasn't seemed at all interested in finding a wife."

Audrey kept her eyes on the road, but she was aware that Naomi was gazing at her.

"So, while all that's going on, you arrive here at our farm and then, suddenly, my brother's also got a lot of things going on in his heart. And I don't think he knows how to sort it all out."

Audrey felt herself blushing, but it was all right. Naomi understood how she felt about Johnny. She had never tried to hide her feelings from her friend.

4

It seemed too hot for a May day. This humidity was something new to her, and Audrey couldn't get used to it. Mexico could be hot, but the higher altitudes where she lived generally were drier. Except for the rainy season which, she remembered, was just about to begin. Then buckets of water poured from the sky, roads were sometimes washed out, and all of life had to be adjusted to the heavy rainfall. The rain was another thing so different from California. But this Ohio humidity was taking a toll on her energy.

She had already ironed a huge stack of tablecloths. She had "sprinkled" them first, according to Mandy's instructions, then pressed them carefully with the flatirons heated on the wood-burning stove in the basement of the farmhouse. The steam rose from the crisp fabric, adding to the moisture already in the air. She'd pulled her hair back into a ponytail to keep the heaviness of its weight off her neck, but tendrils of auburn hair kept escaping, falling around her face. The humidity was adding curl that wasn't normally there. She tried to blow a strand away from her eyes.

I should just pull everything up and put it under a cap like Naomi does, she thought wryly. But she understood that Naomi's covering was more than just an item of fashion or convenience. It would be disrespectful for her to use a cap simply to keep her hair under control.

She set down the iron, smoothed the cloth under one hand, and reached up to tuck another strand of hair behind an ear. Picking up the iron again, she quickly dropped it and drew back her hand. A disgusted grunt escaped.

"Audrey, when will you learn those things are hot? Remember to use the pad!" she scolded.

Her eye caught a movement at the door and she looked up. Johnny stood there. The ornery look in his eye told her that he was trying not to laugh at her.

"Can't get used to these irons." She shook her head and sighed.

"Looks like you've gotten a lot accomplished in spite of it," he replied.

"But I'll have to wear white gloves to Naomi's wedding to hide all the blisters!" she retorted. "Sorry, I'm complaining too much. It's just been … an experience. Learning to use these things."

"I imagine so," he said.

They were both grasping for something to say. It was the first time since her arrival that they had been alone, just the two of them. The awkward silence lasted too long. Finally, he added, "You've worked hard. Really helped Mom. And I know that Naomi is so excited that you're here."

"I was looking forward to coming," she said with a slight, soft smile.

For just a moment, green eyes met blue, then Johnny looked away. "Dad will be wondering if I've disappeared …" and he started up the stairway.

"Bye," said Audrey.

She turned back to the tablecloth lying across the ironing board, smoothed it one more time, and picked up the pad for the iron before also lifting the iron. She realized she was very tired, but she smiled to herself and hummed a little tune as she ran the flatiron over and over a tablecloth already perfectly pressed.

***

She paused at the open barn door, breathing in the aromas of living creatures, their feed, the straw and the hay. All of it pleased her immensely; it reminded her of her family's horse farm in the mountains and of the little village in central Mexico where she had found a place to pour out her love into the lives of children. In those two places, she felt closer to the earth, a good thing, in her mind. At her home in Malibu, too much concrete came between people and the natural world.

She had not yet been to the barn during milking. The twice-daily ritual was something Naomi had often mentioned in letters, and Audrey was hoping to try her hand at it—just once, just to see what it was like. Only Johnny and his father were milking tonight. Naomi and Mandy had too many other things to tend to in the few days before the wedding.

As she stepped forward, three tiny kittens came skittering past. One darted between her feet, and Audrey danced and hopped to avoid stepping on it. Mama cat paid no attention to her offspring; she was sitting about five feet away from Johnny, her eyes on his skillful hands coaxing the milk from a full udder.

Johnny's head touched the side of the black and white cow. He did not see Audrey. But he did know the cat was there, watching and waiting.

In one swift motion, he turned a stream of milk toward mama cat, and in precise, quick reaction, she caught it in her open mouth. The two seemed to know the game well. Mama cat's tongue flicked out to get every drop off her whiskers, and then she sat, still as a statue, again waiting.

"How did you train her to do that?" asked Audrey, now standing close to the cat.

Johnny looked up, surprise on his face.

"You mean this?" he asked, and he directed a stream of white toward Audrey.

She gave a small shriek and jumped back, stepping backward quickly to move out of range. Her green eyes gave him a full glare, half teasing and half threatening. Then she turned, and with exaggerated haughtiness, began walking toward the back of the barn.

A deep bellow came after her.

"No! Stop!" roared Johnny. She heard the wooden stool rattle on the floor and hit the milk pail.

Shocked, she turned, wide-eyed. Johnny stood staring at her, pale and ... was he shaking?

He ignored the trail of milk where all the kittens were now lapping greedily and strode toward Audrey quickly. His hand touched her back, urging her forward, toward the doorway she had come through just a few minutes before.

"Don't. Don't go back there. Stay out of the way of those horses." His voice sounded harsh.

"I ..." She didn't know what to say. She had grown up around horses; she would have been cautious, especially in the presence of animals who did not know her. But Johnny's hand pushed her away from the stalls, toward the door. What had she done? "Johnny, I'm sorry. I didn't know ..."

The color was coming back to his face, and now he seemed angry. His hand dropped from her back, and his words were clipped. "Just stay away from the horses."

And without a backward look at the cows, the overturned milk pail, Audrey, or his father, he walked out of the barn.

5

The valley was filled with a heavy, early morning mist. Johnny walked briskly up the hill toward the woods. He had at least half an hour before his father would be out to start milking.

He had to clear his head. Settle some things. The scene in the barn the night before had shaken him. He had looked up to see Audrey moving back along the alley, toward the same spot where Annie had received that deadly kick from one of the horses. Without even thinking, he had jumped up and shouted a warning.

He had overreacted. Of course Audrey knew how to give horses plenty of room. But when she had turned a bewildered face to him, he realized that the thought that had flashed through his head was, *I cannot lose them both in the same way.*

Why was he thinking of Audrey in that way? Why had he *claimed* her?

He was angry with himself. He had made his decision over a year before. She lived in one world; he in another. They had met in her world, and then he had made the decision to hop on his bike and pedal away as fast as he could. They were not right for each other. He *could not* think of Audrey in that way. He must do something to keep any thoughts of her locked up behind that door in the back corner of his mind.

As he climbed the hill at a pace that left him breathless, he thought of going to his old tree house. At one time, it had been his hideaway, a place where he calmed or straightened his thoughts. But had he outgrown the tree house? He had given his nephew Simon permission to use it, and the boy had made some additions. Still, maybe there, in his old sanctuary, he could put these thoughts about Audrey to rest once and for all.

As he followed the field lane that went up the hill along the fence row, he ascended through the mist and came out above the fog, at the edge of the woods.

He reached the huge old oak tree holding the tree house in its branches and glanced back down toward the barn. The mist had enveloped the buildings below. Behind the eastern hills, the sky was just beginning to lighten.

For some reason, he did not climb the ladder to the tree house. Deep inside, he knew it was not what he needed this morning.

He needed, he thought, to talk to Annie.

In the first year after she was gone, he had often heard Annie's voice. He knew exactly how she would respond in so many instances. When he had first met Audrey and felt that immediate attraction, Annie had teased him. But for a long time now, he had not heard his wife's voice.

"Annie, I have got to talk to you." He listened, waiting. He heard nothing.

He wanted to somehow connect with the calming influence his wife had always had on him. His eyes moved along the ridge, and the white fence around the cemetery seemed to shine in the twilight of morning. Maybe there, where Annie was buried, he could sort out his thoughts.

There, too, lay his grandparents and great-grandparents. Someday Mandy and John would be there. He was the fourth generation to farm this land. Thinking about all who had lived before him and created this farm and the life he now lived made him feel on solid ground—as though he were held firmly and things were somehow unshakeable.

He wanted that. He wanted to feel that he stood on solid ground.

Because Audrey had shaken him.

So he cut through the field, and the wet grass brushed his pants legs. Along the fence line he went, crossing Strawberry Lane, and opening the gate to the graveyard.

As he started toward Annie's grave, a slight movement at the top of the rise caught his eye. A huddled figure sat against the lone tree among the gravestones.

Her back was to him. He recognized the dark blue of his mother's work coat. The coat was much too big for her, though, and she was using it like a poncho, wrapped around her. The auburn hair fell loose on her shoulders. A Bible was on her knees.

For a moment, he was paralyzed. He could not … not now, not here. He would go. Quietly.

But she heard something and turned her face toward him.

She had seen him. Brushing at her cheek, she stood up. He noticed she was in blue jeans, something she had not worn in all the time she'd been with the Millers. She had brought skirts and dresses. He could not help but notice the picture she made with her blue jeans paired with Mandy's coat.

"Good morning, Johnny."

"Good morning," he said gravely.

What more was there to say?

"A cemetery is a good place to sit and reflect and get the proper perspective on my life," she began. Then a concerned look flashed across her face. "Oh, have I intruded? Some cultures would consider this an intrusion—you know, sacred burial grounds and all that. I'm sorry if I've done something offensive by being here."

"No, it's all right."

"Good, because I've been up here several times. I love the early morning light. When I watch the sun come up, I can almost imagine the breaking of a new day of eternity. It's so lovely here. Would they allow me to be buried here someday?"

He was pretty certain that never had an Amish man been asked such a question by such a woman.

She saw his bewilderment.

"I'm joking. I'm joking!"

His relieved mind moved on to something else, something urgent.

"I must apologize for last evening. I want to explain."

"Your father told me, after you left the barn," she said gently. "I'm so sorry. I never intended to trigger painful memories."

"No need to apologize. It wasn't your fault." His voice was raspy. "Many things remind me."

They stood side by side, staring out over the mist-filled valley. Neither knew what to say.

"Look at that," Audrey finally said. "Isn't it beautiful? It's like looking across a gray sea, and the hills over there look like mountains on the other side of the water."

The world below was gone. The fields and the road had disappeared. The Miller houses and the farm buildings didn't exist. They stood in a cemetery, above a sea of clouds. And Audrey was right—the eastern hills looked like mountain peaks jutting up beyond the gray swells of cloud-sea.

He knew that once the sun rose above the line of hills, its brilliance would be blinding. He remembered the first time he had met her, how brilliant the California sun had been that day, how blue the Pacific had shone in the distance. There had not been a cloud in the sky that day. He had been pedaling hard and fast to escape the Amish life and find his new life when her green eyes had caught his and pierced through the darkness of his grief. He remembered the red convertible, flying along roads that twisted through the mountains, the well-tended horse farm, and the one horse that almost kept him in California—or had it been this woman who had almost kept him there?

He closed his eyes and gave a brief shake of his head. He could not think about that.

"Do you miss Mexico?"

"I miss my children. But I'll only be gone two weeks, then I'll be back."

"I remember you said that you want to change the world, one small child at a time."

"Yes, I did say that, didn't I? But I've changed my thinking a bit. On my own in Mexico, I've had more time to focus on reading the Scriptures and getting to know God better. And I've discovered that He doesn't want to change the world. His plan is to eventually do away with this world and create a new one. What God is really interested in is changing people's hearts so that they're ready to live in His new world."

"Annie talked a lot about God transforming people," Johnny said. "She always compared the transformation to the life of a Monarch butterfly. She loved those butterflies. Thought their entire life cycle was a miracle and mirrored what God does with us—He takes worms and changes them into beautiful butterflies."

"Oh! The Monarchs! Oh, Johnny!" She turned to face him, and her eyes were alive. "The Monarchs! Have you ever studied their migration patterns? Millions of them fly thousands and thousands of miles every fall to some place in the Michoacan mountains. No one seems to know where they go, but by the time they fly over and through our village, there are so many of them that it looks like great orange clouds floating overhead. When the butterflies come through, many of the natives believe the butterflies are the spirits of the dead, returning to their homes. It's quite a sight. You'll have to see it sometime."

She stopped abruptly, as though she had just thought of something.

"Well, let's see. What time of the year would that be? I'll need to start a few months early if I'm going in the buggy." Johnny joked.

"I forgot you didn't fly."

"I have often wondered, though, where those butterflies go. Annie would collect the caterpillars, tend them through the chrysalis stage, and then release the butterflies once they emerged. Then they're gone, but they always come back the next summer."

"The interesting thing is that the whole yearly cycle involves four generations," Audrey said. Johnny knew this, but he let her go on. "The fourth generation is the one that travels so far. That generation lives long enough to get to Mexico, over-winter, and then start the trip back north. They die on the way, though, and the next two generations each live only about two weeks and travel a little farther. The third generation completes the journey and lays eggs in the northern habitat and then dies. In the fall, the fourth generation again undertakes the long journey to Mexico. It really is an amazing story. I didn't know anything about Monarchs until last fall when I witnessed the first swarms of them coming over the town."

"There's actually hundreds of them flying together?"

"Thousands. And they're all headed in the same direction. Thus far, no one has discovered where they go, although I'm sure there are some people up higher in the mountains who might know."

"I can't imagine it. But it would be something to see."

Audrey smiled.

"Maybe sometime, Johnny."

The sea of clouds below them had changed. It had not disintegrated, but it was moving upward. Tendrils of gray drifted up the hill, reaching into the cemetery, threading around them. The lines of the gravestones softened. More and more of the world was fading away into the mist.

They stood watching. Silent.

"How long will you stay there?"

"In Mexico? I don't know. Until God moves me elsewhere, I guess. For now, that's where I'm to be. I can't imagine having to disentangle myself from those children's lives, but I guess it will be just like raising a family. The children grow up, leave the nest, and create their own families and lives. But I don't try to look too far into the future. I try to keep my eyes on what God is doing today, and what He wants *me* to be doing as my part of the big plan."

"The big plan?"

"Pointing people toward God. Letting them know that they can have a special relationship with their Creator."

"Are you a missionary?" Johnny asked.

She smiled, and he thought, *That's a happy smile. She's happy with her life.*

"No I don't really think of myself that way. I think of myself as a follower of Jesus Christ, on a mission for Him, and He is using my talents in the circumstances where I find myself. I'm there because my mother built the orphanage and is on the board, and we knew they needed a teacher. So that's where I'm applying the gifts God gave me. You ..." She cast a sidelong glance at Johnny. "You seem to be gifted as a farmer. This must be where God decided to set your shining light."

He gave a nonchalant shrug. "I'm not sure that light is shining very brightly."

She looked at him, and he felt as though she were peering into his soul and there was no way to hide what was there. Her eyes went back to the sky that was still clear above the sea of mist.

"Well, your farm looks like it's doing very well. Naomi says you can coax the land to grow almost anything."

The farm! The mist was thinning now, and Johnny could see the outline of the barn appearing. The world below was emerging again, rising up and reclaiming his thoughts.

"I've got to get back down there for milking. Dad will already be in the barn, wondering where I am."

"I think I'll stay a bit longer," said Audrey. Then, putting on a severely prim look, she added, "Besides, I don't suppose it would look proper for us to come down the hill together just as the sun is coming up."

"I'll see you at breakfast," Johnny said as he started toward the cemetery gate.

She raised her voice slightly to call after him. "Yes, see you at breakfast."

He jogged down the hill, disappearing into the mist.

6

"Have you seen the difference in Johnny?" asked Naomi, as she and Audrey tackled a mound of potatoes piled on the table in the basement kitchen. Every last potato must be peeled, readied for cooking and mashing for the wedding meal.

"The difference?" Audrey asked.

"Oh, come on, surely you've noticed. He's almost his old self. A few jokes this morning, some teasing. He seems to have had a load lightened in some way." Naomi raised her eyebrows at her friend. "Did you have anything to do with that?"

"We had a talk. That's all," said Audrey. She shrugged her shoulders. She had noticed, though.

She was beginning to see the man she had met in California.

***

"I'll wash," Audrey offered as the family rose from the supper table.

The dishes were piled higher than usual. Naomi's three older sisters had been at the Miller home all day, helping with wedding preparations, and their husbands and children had also arrived at supper time. Mandy had insisted on a large family dinner, and that meant Johnny's older brother Jonas and his family would also be invited. And then Paul must also be included, since he, too, would be family by the end of the week.

Somehow, even in the midst of wedding activity, a sumptuous meal had been prepared, complete with coffee and pie to end the evening. The happiness surrounding the upcoming nuptials had infused everyone, even the brothers-in-law, who Audrey had at first thought to be quite stern and serious. There was much laughter at the supper table, and Audrey quietly watched, listened, and enjoyed it all. This was family life as she had never known or imagined it.

She wanted to stay in the thick of it. So she offered to wash the dishes, even though the stacks were formidable.

"And we shall let you wash," said Mandy. The men were drifting away toward the living room, but the sisters all grabbed dish towels and stood ready as Audrey stationed herself at the sink.

She heard Johnny's voice raised above the hubbub.

"Audrey, you know what they're doing, don't you? They're testing you … to see if you're ready to get married," he said.

She heard the light, teasing tone, but raised her eyes to him in alarm.

"What?" She felt a flush come into her cheeks.

"They're testing you. Around here, there's a saying that you aren't properly prepared to get married until you can wash dishes fast enough to keep four Amish ladies busy drying. I've seen my sisters do dishes, and believe me, you won't keep up with them."

"Don't listen to him," said Naomi. "We're thinking nothing of the sort."

Audrey gave Johnny another look; he was grinning at her.

Her hand came up out of the suds, holding the dishcloth. She gave it a slight squeeze and shake, and then fired the soggy ball at him. His hand shot out, grabbed the wet cannonball, and heaved it right back at her. She ducked, and the dishcloth landed back in the dishwater, sending a fine spray of sudsy bubbles into the air.

The sisters laughed gleefully. "She's too fast for you, Johnny," said the oldest, Martha.

"Or else you're getting slower," teased Naomi.

*   *   *

It was Wednesday, the day before the wedding. Audrey was on the road to Stevenson. She had offered to pick up Bill McCollum, who was flying into the Stevenson airport in his private jet.

Johnny was busy with last-minute preparations in the barn, where the morning service would be held. He and his brother, Jonas, also moved two beds from John and Mandy's big house into his own smaller house. The beds were set up in the room that had once been Annie's sewing room. McCollum and his pilot would stay with Johnny, in the newly created guest room.

He kept an eye on the driveway. He didn't want to miss Bill's arrival.

He had met Bill McCollum as he had pedaled his bicycle through Texas. The big man had an equally big reputation and wide circle of influence—he owned a successful farm-equipment manufacturing company. More important to Bill was his giving—his primary goal in business seemed to be to earn more money so that he could pour more funds into missions around the world. Bill had crossed Johnny's path at a time when Johnny desperately needed certainty—certainty of Heaven and God's hand in his life. Then, after Johnny's bicycle accident, Bill had been the first one at the hospital, and he had come often during Johnny's long recuperation.

However, the pilot who flew McCollum's jet was a stranger to Johnny. He had flown Naomi home from Corpus Christi after her stay with Johnny at the hospital (an event that had shocked Johnny—he had thought his father would forbid Naomi's flying), and the Millers had invited him to stay the night with them. They had all liked the pilot very much, and Naomi had also invited him to her wedding. The only other thing Johnny knew about him was that he was a black man, a fact that had apparently caused a stir when he stepped off the jet at the Stevenson airport and then climbed into a van to drive off with Paul and Naomi and stay in an Amish home.

Audrey had left for Stevenson shortly after the noon meal. She had still not returned by suppertime. The airport was only 14 miles away. No one else at the supper table seemed to find it strange that she was not yet back with her two passengers. The conversation at the supper table was directed by Mandy and Naomi, going over details of the next day, making certain everything was ready. Johnny, though, kept wondering, *What could have happened to delay them?*

When the headlights finally turned into the driveway, he felt relief wash over him, and he hurried out to meet the occupants of the car.

Audrey was laughing as she opened her door and stepped out. Bill unfolded his long frame from the back seat just as Johnny reached the side of the car. Johnny was ready to extend his hand, but Bill wrapped him in a bear hug.

"Johnny, my friend! It is good to see you!" The deep voice boomed out over the quiet, dusky valley. "We have a lot of catching up to do."

"Sorry we're so late," Audrey inserted. "We, uh, we spent some time wandering around in circles."

"You were lost?" asked Johnny incredulously.

On the opposite side of the car, a tall man had emerged from the front passenger seat.

"Oh, no. Not lost," Bill answered. "We just couldn't quite get our bearings. I'm afraid I'm the cause of it all. I asked Audrey if we could drive by a piece of land I have an interest in, and I thought I had good directions—but it seems the person who gave me those directions forgot to mention one or two turns. We eventually gave up, and a few kind locals had to point us toward Milford."

"And by then, it was getting so late that I knew supper would be finished here, and everyone is so busy that I didn't want you to bother about feeding us," added Audrey, "so we decided to stop for supper. That little restaurant in Milford has really good food."

"Oh, but we had a great adventure anyway," said the tall man, coming around the car and extending his hand to Johnny. "I'm Josh Richardson. Audrey's been a good tour guide, even though she claims to know little about this area. We did have some fun in spite of everything, didn't we?"

Josh grinned at Audrey, who ducked her head and giggled.

By this time, Naomi, Mandy, and John were all outside to greet the guests. John and Bill shook hands heartily. Johnny was surprised to feel his eyes fill with water as he watched the two older men grasp hands—these two men who had been such strong towers of strength and wisdom in guiding his own wandering life.

"Well, let's get you settled," he said. Audrey had opened the trunk of the car, and Johnny pulled out the two bags and started toward his house.

The two men said goodnight to the family and followed him.

"See you tomorrow," Audrey called after them.

The three were all in high spirits, and Johnny felt a small irritation that he had been worrying about them while they had been having such a good time.

7

Audrey shifted her body, trying to hold herself in a more comfortable position on the hard, narrow bench—but also not wanting her discomfort to be noticed.

The Millers had assured her that she would not have to sit through the entire morning of preaching that would precede the actual ceremony of marriage; many English people, Naomi had told her, waited to slip into the wedding until all the initial preaching was nearing an end and the time for the actual marriage of the two young people had arrived. But Audrey had declined that plan; she wanted the full experience of an Amish wedding. She would sit through the entire morning.

Naomi had just smiled at her friend and said, "Okay."

Now, Audrey wondered if that had been a foolish decision. Since the preachers weren't speaking English, she had understood nothing of what had been said over the last three hours, and her body was beginning to feel as though it were fossilizing into one position.

She was too warm, too. The large area in the barn that had been swept as clean as Mandy's kitchen was filled with rows of benches that were filled with people, the men on one side and the women on the other. She had chosen a pink blouse with long sleeves and a mid-calf, soft gray skirt. The long sleeves had seemed more appropriate, but now she wished she would have settled for three-quarter sleeves. That would have been at least a bit cooler.

She had pulled her hair up into a swirl of auburn at the back of her head. The warm day's humidity had pulled out curls again, and some had escaped the pins. Oh, well, there was nothing to be done about it.

But this pink blouse. The pink was too intense. Looking around at the somber dresses of the other women and the black suits of the men, she felt entirely out of place. She had not wanted to be an obvious outsider. She'd debated a long time about the clothes she brought to Ohio. But now she was certain—the pink was a mistake.

She had even put on the skirt and blouse one evening earlier in the week and asked Naomi if the outfit would be acceptable for the wedding.

"Is it all right? I don't want to stand out in the crowd," she had said to the bride-to-be.

Naomi's eyes and smile shone with tenderness for her friend.

"Audrey, I'm sorry to tell you, but there is no way you're going to 'blend in.' But that's all right. We don't expect you to look like us. And," she added, eyes twinkling, "you look beautiful."

Naomi was beautiful, too. Her wedding dress was a soft blue. She sat in a line of young women, facing a line of young men that included Paul, her soon-to-be husband.

They've barely looked at each other all morning, thought Audrey. Not understanding a word of the preaching, she had spent plenty of time observing the people around her.

Like every other Amish man there, Johnny wore a black suit with simple lines, no collar, and, of course, no tie. His hair was neatly combed; his beard was just beginning to touch the front of his shirt. He looked very solemn. *And very Amish,* she thought. She could barely see the man she had once known in California.

Her mind went to Johnny and Annie. This was how they had been married. They had sat through a morning like this. And this was how Johnny would someday take another woman to be his wife.

The entire wedding was so different from every other wedding she had attended—as different as Malibu, California, was from this quiet farm in Ohio. The bride and groom never touched; there was never a kiss, no rings, no flowers or candles or wedding march. Yet as Audrey watched when Paul and Naomi finally stood and—apparently—the preacher finally married them, Audrey felt a great satisfaction that here were two, now united as one before God and their community.

She couldn't help it. A huge smile spread across her face. She wanted to applaud, too, but she was able to stifle that impulse.

***

Somewhere between the barn and the big house, where tables and chairs filled every square inch of space, a transformation had taken place. As Audrey, Bill, and Josh took their seats at a table for the wedding dinner, Audrey saw that Naomi and Paul had put off the solemnity and were greeting friends with smiles and laughter. Naomi's cheeks were bright pink, and she was brimming with happiness. The men, who had looked so formal and reserved in their black suits, had relaxed.

The house hummed with activity. Servers, who were all dressed in the same color of dresses or shirts, glided among the tables, bringing dishes heaped with food.

Paul and Naomi and their attendants were seated at the bridal table. Johnny was seated there, too. He had taken off his coat, and Audrey thought he looked very handsome in his black vest and white shirt. As she took her seat between Bill and Josh, Johnny's eyes met hers, and he gave her a smile.

"You're looking beautiful today, young lady," said Bill, as he passed a bowl of steaming mashed potatoes to Audrey.

"Thank you," she murmured. Even though they were mashed, she was sure that she recognized some of those potatoes as ones that had gone through her cramping fingers when she and the sisters had spent a morning peeling them all.

Then Josh chimed in with a question, and Audrey was lost in the flow of food and conversations. Other English people were also seated at their table, and introductions were made, explanations brought forth about how each knew Paul and Naomi, and stories told. In the midst of good company, Audrey was keenly aware of two things.

The first was Josh's attention to her. He was not rude to the others; he was well-spoken and his conversation with others at the table was interested and engaging. But when he turned to Audrey, she noticed that he had more than a polite interest in everything she had to say. They talked about her work at the orphanage and about his opportunities working for Bill McCollum; he was only a few years older than her, but he flew all over the world, overseeing the distribution of funds and implementation of mission programs. She had to admit, Josh's life sounded fascinating.

And the second thing that she could not miss was that Johnny also noticed. She caught his glance once or twice, but he immediately looked away. A bit flustered by Josh's attention, wondering what Johnny was thinking, and still convinced her pink blouse stood out too much in this crowd, Audrey felt something that was rare for her—an uneasy discomfort.

8

After all the people and activity of the day before, Friday morning seemed calm and peaceful. Even the cows at milking seemed to sense that the wedding was over, and life was going back to normal.

Except that Naomi was no longer at the breakfast table. Bill McCollum and Josh Richardson had replaced her. And they were enjoying Mandy's breakfast tremendously.

"I'm going to be meeting the real estate agent today to look at that 40 acres," said Bill.

"You're buying land here?" asked John.

"Yes, I'm thinking of building a factory right here in the middle of farming country. It's quite a different environment than our factory in Texas, but I think it would be a strategic location. Taxes here are relatively low. It's rural, but near enough to good supply lines. How about labor? I notice that the Amish have a large presence here. Would they be willing to work in a factory?"

"They will," answered John. "It's true, our numbers are growing. And there's only so much farm land left. Many young Amish men are seeking work elsewhere. And they will be reliable, hard workers, on the whole."

"I've been in touch with a local realtor, and he says this is a prime piece of land. We tried to find it the day we flew into town, but we were, uh, unsuccessful."

Audrey rolled her eyes at this, and Josh grinned at her.

"So I'm going to meet him and walk the land today. Audrey, are you free to drive us?"

Audrey looked at Mandy.

"Of course, go ahead," said Mandy. "I'm not planning on working too hard today. Just recuperating."

"All right. What time do you want to leave?"

And so the three guests were off again, and the Miller farm left to its day-after-wedding quiet.

***

Supper was over. Johnny sat at his kitchen table, idly flipping through a stack of mail. He had been too busy the last few days to pay attention to the envelopes and flyers. Even now, as he sorted through the pile, his mind was elsewhere.

One return address did catch his attention, though. It was another check from Sydney.

What was he going to do with it?

On his bicycle trip, he had met Sydney at a commune and donated a $20 bill to Sydney's fledgling clothing-design business. Sydney had been intrigued by Johnny's Amish pants—the "barn-door" style—and had decided to incorporate the ideas into his own line of pants for both men and women. Johnny knew nothing about the fashion scene, especially in California and the big cities, but apparently Sydney's designs of "Johnny BarnDoors" were catching on and Sydney's business was doing well. He had promised Johnny a cut of the profits, and for months Johnny had been receiving astonishingly big checks. He had thought nothing of it when Sydney asked to sketch his pants; he had even been amused at the designer's enthusiasm. But now, back in his own environment, he felt embarrassed that out there in the world, people were wearing copies of his clothes, paying big money for them, and considering themselves quite stylish.

He was glad for Sydney's success, but what was to be done with this money?

He didn't open the envelope and sighed as he laid it aside. He'd just deposit it as he had done with all the previous checks.

The weekly paper was there. Another envelope was from Annie's parents in Indiana. He and Annie had been married such a short time that Johnny felt he had never really gotten to know the Yoders well. They had kept in touch with him after Annie's death, sending him short letters with family news, and he still felt a kinship with them. The familiar handwriting and their return address, though, reminded Johnny of the grief the Yoders were now dealing with, and he did not open it.

He did not open any of the mail. It could all wait.

He carried the newspaper with him to the chair and settled in. But his mind could not focus on the words in front of his eyes. The light outside had almost completely faded. *Had they been lost yet again? What was delaying them?*

Finally he heard the car in the driveway. Three doors opened and shut. He heard Audrey call out a *goodnight*, and in seconds Bill and Josh were at the door.

"Good trip?" Johnny asked.

"Yes, we had quite the day," Bill said. "I'm very happy about it. The owner spent quite a while bargaining with me—seems he somehow got wind of an oil-rich Texan being interested in his property, and he thought he was going to get every dollar he could. But it looks like the deal will go through. It's a beautiful piece of land. I'm almost sorry that I'm putting a factory on it."

"Yours will be a first for our area," replied Johnny. "I suppose there will be both benefits and disadvantages to having big business come to our community."

"Well, I'm hoping, my friend, that you and your father will help me navigate my way here. I'll need wise advice as we build and go forward," said Bill.

"We'll help you where we can," promised Johnny.

Josh had been sitting quietly, listening to the conversation. He seemed fidgety, though. Now he rose, went to the kitchen window, and looked over toward the big house.

"I wonder if they're still up?" he said.

"If the light's on in the living room, someone will be up," Johnny told him.

Josh glanced at his watch.

"It's not really that late. Think I'll see if Audrey wants to take a walk. We spent the whole day just sitting and waiting ..."

And he was gone.

Johnny and Bill sat silently for a moment. Bill had taken off his big Stetson and laid it on his knee. He was fingering the brim thoughtfully. This was an unusual moment—when Bill was quiet, not booming into whatever space his large body had also invaded.

This was the first opportunity, Johnny realized, that he had time to speak with Bill privately. They had been surrounded by people ever since Bill had arrived.

"You know," Johnny began, "I don't think I ever thanked you for everything you did for my family. But most of all, I'm thankful that you put up that cross. If I had never found it and met you there—well, I'm not sure where I'd be today."

"God drew you there. I believe that. God works in our lives even when we aren't aware of it. And you know—I told you my story—you know that the cross is what made all the difference in my life, too. I'd be a homeless drunk on the streets right now, if it weren't for God's intervention in my life," said Bill.

"Yes," said Johnny thoughtfully. "The assurance I found there that day was exactly what I needed at the time."

"And you, my man—you amazed us all when you walked out of that hospital in Corpus Christi."

Johnny grinned. "Well, I'm pretty amazed myself, when I look back now and think about what I did. My body was in such bad shape, I don't know how I even got out of town."

"Miracles. They still happen," said Bill.

"I agree! I had a miracle of healing on the walk home. There was a man, drowning in the Mississippi River—" Johnny stopped as he thought about what had happened the night he met River Man.

Bill leaned forward in the chair, his eyes brighter.

"Tell me about it."

9

Johnny was silent for a long moment, thinking back over the events of his bicycle ride across the Southwest. So much had happened. Where should the story start?

"You know that when I met you, I was searching for two things: a way to put my life back together after Annie died and assurance of things I had always been taught but was no longer sure I believed. Did God really love me? Did He care about my life? Why did He allow that accident to claim Annie's life? I was full of doubt and confusion.

"Then someone told me where to find your cross—the cross you had built—and when I pedaled by and decided to stop, you were also there. We talked a long while, and after you left, I stayed at the cross and experienced an amazing assurance flow through me. I sat there, and could almost feel the blood of Christ wash over me. I felt cleansed and strengthened and assured of God's love and care.

"But my bicycle accident set me back. I was so angry—" Johnny caught himself. Could he explain why he was so angry? Could he tell Bill that he had actually been at Heaven's door with Annie, but then he was sent back to earth, ripped away from Annie again?

"They say I died. I was so badly injured that my body felt totally useless. I thought for a while I would never walk again. My mind didn't work right, either. Many days, I was certain I was going crazy. Well, you know what shape I was in. You were there at the hospital."

Bill gave a smile and nodded.

"Yes, I remember. But the day that we prayed for your healing, I felt the power of God absolutely explode in that room!"

"But I didn't," said Johnny. "I didn't *feel* God. I didn't know if He was there or not, or if He even cared. Not only had I lost Annie, I had now lost use of my body and my mind. I was angry and bitter."

He took a deep breath.

"And then, after I walked away from the hospital—*escaped* from the hospital—I fell even lower. The physical pain was overwhelming, and the mental anguish seemed paralyzing. I used the pain medication and alcohol to try to escape. I had some very black days.

"One day I stood on the bank of the Mississippi River and screamed at God. I wanted to know why he had forced me to live. I truly wanted to die, to be gone from the body that had me trapped.

"But at the same moment, a man was drowning in the river. I heard him call to God for help. *He* wanted to live. Bill, I don't know how I did it. I could barely walk, and I'm not a strong swimmer, but somehow I managed to get that man out of the river."

Johnny was transported back to the scene on the riverbank. He had built a fire to warm and dry the stranger. They had sat there, in the circle of light from the fire with the dark night encircling them, and had a strange conversation.

"The man never told me much about himself, not even his name. I think of him now as River Man. But he seemed to be able to read my thoughts. He said that God had brought me there, at the right moment to save him. I said I had just happened to be there, but River Man believed that there's no such thing as coincidence. *God has His purpose in everything*, he said. I told him I couldn't see God's purpose in everything; I told him how I had lost Annie, and he asked me, at one point, if I loved Annie more than I loved Jesus. That caused me to think. We talked about Christ bringing new life—just as you and I did, Bill—and River Man reminded me that it's like a kernel of wheat—it is planted and must die so that it can produce brand new life."

Johnny's throat tightened. Could he say the next words? He spoke, more quietly.

"During that hour with River Man, I realized I was moving with absolutely no pain. And I was remembering everything ... *everything*, Bill!"

He felt the tears in his eyes.

"It's impossible to explain and maybe impossible to believe, but it was a healing of my body and my mind. As though God gave me a new life, somehow, miraculously."

"I believe every word of it, my friend," boomed Bill, sounding triumphant, and striking one palm with a fist. "Our God does things like that!"

The things River Man and Johnny had talked about that night were never far from Johnny's thoughts, but telling the story to someone else, hearing his own words hang in the air, filled Johnny with a new sense of awe of what God had done.

He let his head fall back against the chair.

"I believe God does have His purposes in everything, even the terrible, painful things in this life. I believe that, Bill. But I just can't always see it. I don't always *feel* it. I still have many questions."

"That's what faith is all about, Johnny," said Bill. "Walking ahead, trusting what God says, even though we can't see or feel evidence of it."

"I have to tell you that—"

They both turned their heads quickly as the kitchen door opened, accompanied by a crash.

"Oh, I'm so sorry!" Josh was there, scrambling to retrieve two long walking sticks that had stood in the corner behind the door but were now lying on the floor.

"It's all right," said Johnny, rising and walking to the kitchen. "That happens to me sometimes, too. I suppose I should find a better place for these."

He took both sticks from Josh's hands, and carried them back to the living room.

"Here," he said, handing both to Bill. "I keep them—to remind me."

Josh looked from one to the other and knew he had walked into the middle of a conversation. He sat down without a word.

Bill examined the walking sticks, running his hand the length of each, holding each a bit closer to examine the carvings.

"That one—the one with the mountain and sun—that was given to me by another patient at the hospital. The second one, with the cross, was carved by River Man while we sat and talked that night. I didn't realize what he was doing until after he walked away. I thought he was just smoothing out the roughness on a stick I was using. I found the carvings the next morning."

Johnny remembered the moment he had realized what River Man had done to the mesquite branch he had picked up and used as a walking stick. Where before there had been only rough edges and irritating bumps, the bare, beautiful wood now displayed the graceful shape of a cross. At the base of the cross lay a sheaf of wheat. In careful and minute detail, River Man's knife had captured the long, flowing lines of the stalks and the heavy fullness of each ripe head. The detail was so exquisite that Johnny could almost feel the weight of the grain in his hand, remembering moments he had stood in his own wheat fields checking the coming harvest. Looking more closely, he had seen the outline of a butterfly resting at the bottom of the sheaf.

He could not have put into words what he had felt as he discovered the carvings, but the symbols resonated deep in his soul.

He had kept both walking sticks. To the second, the one with his story carved into it, he had applied a finish that enhanced the rich grain and reddish hues. It was beautiful, but Johnny remembered what a rough, unyielding piece of wood it had once been.

"While River Man was carving, he was talking about stories, the stories of our lives."

Johnny paused, not quite knowing how to explain what he felt. He had never said the words aloud to anyone. Then he plunged ahead.

"I've always felt that he somehow carved my story into that one stick, but I'm not sure I know the whole story. I keep them both here, in plain sight, to remind me. Because … I guess I'm still waiting to know the whole story."

"Faith. Walk in faith, Johnny," repeated Bill.

Johnny was suddenly aware that Josh was sitting there, and that he had been over to see Audrey. The reminder called forth a small uneasiness. He was no longer by the fire on the banks of the Mississippi. In a moment, his train of thought had been derailed. He fumbled for something to say.

"Well, what's on the schedule for you two tomorrow?"

Josh spoke first.

"I'd like to get back out to the airport in Stevenson and check on a few things. We'll be flying home on Sunday. Audrey's offered me the use of her car."

"And I think I might just hire on as a farmhand for the day, if you and your father need any help," Bill said with a grin. "There's no more to do right now with the real estate deal. I'd like to see more of your daily operation, get more advice from John about locating here, and definitely see that famous one-bottom plow you've got."

Johnny laughed. Bill's equipment company had made that plow. He wasn't sure how this Texan would find working on a small, hilly Ohio farm, but it would be interesting to work beside him.

And he felt a small pleasure knowing that Audrey had offered the car to Josh. To drive himself.

10

One place the big Texan did not fit was in Johnny's old tree house.

To Johnny's amazement, Bill had spotted the hideaway in the tall oak at the edge of the woods while they were walking toward the barn the next morning.

"Is that a hunting stand up there on the hill?" Bill had asked.

"That's what it was a few generations ago," said Johnny. "But I claimed it when I was 10, added walls, windows, and roof, and made it my own private sanctuary."

"You must have been an enterprising young man."

"Energetic, I guess. Several life-changing events took place up there," mused Johnny.

"Oh?" Bill caught the tone of Johnny's voice. "Is it still private? Could I get an invitation to see it?"

Johnny eyed his friend's height and bulk.

"I'm not sure you'd fit." They both laughed. "But, of course, you're welcome. I rarely go up there these days. As a matter of fact, I think my nephew Simon has claimed it."

"Will he care if we take a look?"

And so they climbed the hill to the tree house. Bill did, indeed, have to take off his hat and duck his head to enter the doorway. He seemed to fill the interior, but the roof was tall enough that he could stand straight. He looked around.

The painted beer bottles were still there, stuffed with notes to God and bearing Johnny's proposal to Annie and her jubilant answer. Johnny's old books and the rug Annie had put on the floor were reminders of another time. Bill paused in front of a paper tacked to the wall. It was the note Johnny had written the day he had turned control of his life over to Jesus. As Bill pondered the note, Johnny's eyes lingered on the last line: *I am going to follow Jesus.*

How well had he kept that promise? Was he following? Was there more he should be doing? What did God really want from him?

"I feel," said Bill, as he turned to his host, "that I might have invaded sacred territory. But thank you for showing this to me."

"You're welcome," said Johnny, not knowing what else to add. Then he had a thought.

"Come outside. Take a look at the view."

Carefully, they maneuvered around each other and exited to stand on the floor that Johnny had left extended beyond the walls to create a narrow deck. Above them was a dome of deep blue without a single cloud. The valley lay below, the fields beginning to show early-summer green. The barn, houses, and shop at the foot of the hill shone white in the bright sunshine. They could see Mandy in her garden. Audrey came from the house and talked with her briefly before then going on to the barn.

"You know," Bill began, "that young lady cares a great deal for you. She was at your side almost immediately after the accident. And she stayed there for weeks, even though you didn't know who she was or why she was there."

"She stayed to help Naomi," Johnny offered. He did not want to talk about this.

"Maybe," said Bill, looking away from Johnny toward the hills on the other side of the valley. Johnny could hear the smile in his voice, even though he was also looking at the horizon, not at

Bill. "She was telling us about her work in the orphanage in Mexico. Her heart has been captured by those little ones. But it's pretty obvious she has a heart for you, too, my friend."

"We were friends. But nothing more than that. She lives in another world."

"She seems to be enjoying this life here."

"But this is only temporary. Becoming a part of this life—that would be something quite different."

"All right, we won't talk about it. But let me give you one bit of advice, my friend. Never try to guess a woman's mind. You'll never know what she's thinking unless you ask her."

Johnny was beginning to feel irritated.

"Maureen wrote to me that you found her son and brought him home," he said.

Johnny's nurse at the hospital, Maureen, had been praying that her son would be found—he had been missing in Viet Nam for two years.

"God did it. We just provided the tools for Him to work."

"That must be quite a story—how you found him and rescued him. And I can imagine the homecoming." Johnny remembered Maureen's small house, filled with memories of the past and hope that she would someday welcome her son home.

"It was a wonderful homecoming," agreed Bill. "You know what it reminded me of? It was a perfect illustration of what Jesus did for us—came right into enemy territory to rescue us who were prisoners and bring us home to God."

Johnny heard the change in Bill's voice and he glanced at his tall friend. There were tears in the Texan's eyes.

"I will never stop being grateful that He rescued me from the destructive cycle I was in. That's why I will follow wherever He leads me for the rest of my life. And I never imagined the things He had in store once I decided to do that. It's been an exciting journey. I see from that note on the wall inside that you've made that determination, too."

"Yes," replied Johnny. "I wrote that several years ago, but it seems like it all happened in a different life."

"A different life? But you're right back here—"

"I know, but things are not the same."

Bill contemplated Johnny's confession.

"Do you suppose God could have something else in mind for you? My experience has always been that when I'm feeling restless, God is getting ready to move me on to something different."

"I'm Amish. I'm a farmer. My place is here."

"When you wrote that note … What does following Jesus mean to you, Johnny?"

Johnny gave a grunt.

"To tell you the truth, I've been wondering that myself."

They were both quiet, watching the scenes in the valley below.

"You have quite a farm here. How much?"

"How much land? One hundred twenty acres. I'm the fourth generation on this farm."

"Might God have bigger fields for you to seed and harvest, my friend? Might God have a life for you with boundaries far bigger than 120 acres?"

"I was convinced this was the right choice for me. This is the way I chose to live."

"What if God has other plans for you?"

Must this man constantly poke and prod?

"Bill, I really don't think it's possible. My land is here. My place is here. This is the right place for me."

His words came out more sharply than he intended, but he saw that Bill understood. The talk turned to soil, planting, and farm equipment. Safe subjects. But Johnny was relieved when they climbed down the ladder and went back down the hill.

11

Early Sunday morning, Mandy and John were at Johnny's door to say goodbye to their guests. They were ready to walk over Strawberry Hill to church services. Hearty handshakes were exchanged all around, and both Texans received an invitation to return any time. Bill assured them he would be back soon.

Johnny was dressed, too, ready for church. He left soon after his parents. Bill and Josh were packing to leave. Audrey would take them to the airport just after lunch, before the Millers had returned from their church service. Mandy, of course, assured them there was plenty of food in her refrigerator and they could help themselves to anything they found.

The service seemed much longer than usual. Johnny could not focus on what his father was preaching. He stayed for lunch, but left soon after, not lingering to visit with the other men. At home, though, he found he was equally restless. His guests were gone. He could not read. He did not want to take a walk. His body seemed on edge, and he could not nap.

What does it mean to follow Jesus? The question kept echoing in his mind. He wished he had a firm answer, because this really was his desire. But how could he know what it meant for him?

He did not have an answer. He admitted that to himself now. Surely it meant following Jesus' teaching, living as He had taught.

Was that it? But *following* ... Did it mean, literally, that one had to be *moving, going?* Like Audrey—going someplace?

He'd started out on that bike ride because he had felt he *had* to be going somewhere, finding something. He had hoped for a new life. Hoped to find a way to deal with the loss of Annie. When he had left, his father had told him, *You'll never find anything out there better than here.*

What had that bike ride accomplished? Pain. A broken body and mind. No, those weren't the only results of his ride. He'd had another life offered to him, a completely different life. He had also found the assurance that he longed for, the assurance that Jesus had, indeed, rescued and saved him. He'd met Bill, he'd met Maureen, he'd met Audrey.

"Bill seems to think that all of that is for a reason." He heard one part of his mind actually voicing the thought.

And what could the reason be? To give me assurance? To save Maureen's son? To bring me back home to farm?

The questions made Johnny uncomfortable.

He did know one thing. If he had pledged to follow Jesus, he'd better find out what that meant. He'd better know who Jesus was and what He asked of his followers.

For all of his life, Johnny had heard *about* Jesus. The one who could save him from hell. The one who could transform a life. The one who came to earth to show mankind who God was.

But who was Jesus?

Johnny could not say that he knew Jesus very well.

Maybe that's the first step.

He decided to read the Gospels—four books about Jesus, all written from different perspectives, by very different people. Which one to read first?

Might as well start in the beginning. With the first one.

He sat down in Annie's chair, picked up his Bible, and opened it to the book written by Matthew.

***

Johnny's reading that afternoon had not gone very far before he realized, with a start, that he had also not known Matthew very well. Turns out that man was a bit of a scoundrel and alienated from the "good" religious people. He was very likely involved in some shady business deals. Yet Jesus asked Matthew to join His circle of friends. And when Jesus drew criticism for that, He had replied, "This is why I came—to heal those who know they are sick."

That was me, thought Johnny, as he read. *Sick, needing help, and knowing it.*

And Jesus did heal. He healed sick bodies and sick souls. He changed lives. And then, when the tide of popularity turned against Jesus, He was falsely accused, arrested, and condemned to die.

At this point, Johnny remembered another portion of Scripture that he had often heard quoted: *Jesus' suffering*, Isaiah had written, *healed us all.*

Johnny had tears in his eyes. The words were too blurry to read. He raised his eyes to the window. Dusk was falling.

He got up and lit the gas lamps. At the kitchen window, he looked over at the big house, wondering if Audrey had returned.

He sat down again and read the last chapter of Matthew's book. It closed with an account of Jesus, alive again, saying farewell to His disciples. He was returning to Heaven. Johnny's eyes caught part of a verse that he did not remember ever seeing before: *but some of them doubted.*

What? Jesus' friends, who had seen Him die, now stood in front of Him alive and talking with them—and they still doubted! Perhaps his own doubts and questions were not a terrible sin but were only the natural result of a human mind trying to grapple with things too big, too heavenly, to understand. He heard Bill's voice, *Walk in faith, Johnny.*

And there also was the well-known verse, the mission Jesus gave to His disciples: Go into the world and make disciples of all nations. *What does that mean for me? Is that command for me?*

He heard a car swing into the driveway.

12

On Monday morning, Johnny hitched Joyce up to the road cart. It would be a longer-than-usual trip for the horse—the destination was Stevenson. Johnny realized he could have asked Audrey to drive him to town, but he decided that would not be wise. He could have called another driver, too, but then Audrey would have, in her practical way, suggested they take her car. No, the best thing would be to take Joyce and the road cart.

He had offered to return several documents to the title office for his dad. Actually, he was looking forward to a long drive alone. There had been so much activity the last few days and so many things had invaded the peace and structure of his life that he needed time to think, time to breathe, time to regain his balance. He was counting on the feel of the reins in his hand, the steady sound of Joyce's hooves on the asphalt, and the leisurely travel through familiar countryside to all have a calming effect on him.

He had just climbed into the cart and picked up the reins when Audrey came running out of the house, waving at him.

"Wait!" she called. He sat patiently and waited until she stood beside him. "Can I go with you?"

She stood beside the cart, breathless, with shining eyes. "I've been here over a week, and I still haven't had a buggy ride. Can I ride along? Please?"

What could he tell her? *No, I can't have you near me? Because I don't know what to say to you or how to keep you at arm's length?*

"Climb up," he said.

She climbed up to the seat beside him.

"Thank you, thank you!"

They turned onto the road. Johnny saw three children walking toward them. He recognized Martha's three youngest. They waved and grinned and called greetings to Audrey as the cart clattered past them. The entire Miller family liked Audrey, but the children loved her; she had won their hearts with her rapt attention to their stories and her enthusiastic participation in their games. In the few days she had been at the farm, she had always taken time to shower attention and affection on the children.

They soon passed the little one-room school.

"Is this where Annie taught?" Audrey asked.

"Yes, this is where I first met her."

Audrey had more questions about Amish schools. Of course, she was a teacher. Johnny answered, while thinking to himself that he was glad school was over for the year and no one was there to see them passing by.

Then Milford loomed ahead of them. Oh, he could have avoided the town; but that would have meant traveling the dirt back roads, where they would meet many more of his Amish neighbors and acquaintances. He chose the town, instead.

Reaching up, he pulled his hat down just a little further. He decided to keep the conversation focused on safe subjects, but he was conscious that their exchange was stilted and unnaturally formal. He tried to ignore the stares of folks on the sidewalk.

But then, maybe they weren't staring at this odd couple; maybe they were only staring at Audrey, a strikingly beautiful English woman riding in an Amish road cart. Maybe they weren't wondering about the *odd couple* in the road cart.

Audrey was ignoring the awkwardness of his attempts at banter. Her bubbly nature was seizing this opportunity for adventure, and she was making the most of it. She waved cheerfully at people who acknowledged them.

Stick to safe subjects. The school, where he had attended for eight years. The feed mill, where they took their grain and he bought his first flock of chicks. The general store. As they rode through Milford, he told insignificant stories about the town and businesses. They passed the restaurant, and it was Audrey's turn to comment. He was reminded that she, Bill, and Josh had eaten there one day.

She wanted to stop everywhere, just for a moment, just to get a flavor of life here, she said. But he told her they had too far to go, and a horse and cart didn't cover the miles as fast as her car.

She seemed satisfied then to sit back and enjoy the sunshine and scenery. She talked about the orphanage, and how much she missed "her" children.

"But I am still thinking about Annie's little girl. Her parents and sister are suddenly gone. How does a little child cope with that? Do you know who is caring for her?" Audrey asked, in an unexpected turn to a serious subject.

"She's with her grandparents, Annie's parents. For the time being, at least. I don't know if there are other relatives who might adopt her or not," replied Johnny. "Annie had another sister, the youngest, but she and her husband left the Amish and moved to North Carolina, and they don't have much communication with the Yoder family, so I doubt whether they would be in the picture."

"Is it true that when an Amish person leaves the Amish church, the family practically disowns him or her?" Audrey turned to him with sober eyes.

"I'm not sure *disowns* is the best word. We call it *shunning* or *miting*. It's a form of church discipline. It's meant to bring a wayward person back into the church. If a person is being mited, he can't eat with the family—or anyone in the church—and often is not included in family activities."

Audrey was silent. Johnny imagined that her tender heart was grieving this. She did not like discord or pain. And since she knew so little of the Amish way of life, it would be hard for her to see that discipline was meant for the good of the one being mited.

"So if Naomi and Paul left the Amish church, they would not be welcome in your house?" she asked quietly.

Johnny glanced at her in alarm.

"Paul and Naomi will never leave."

"But, what if ... ?" she persisted. "What if they did?"

Johnny was silent for a moment, thinking about what would happen in his own family.

"Aren't those rules ever lifted? Don't they allow for any leeway or grace?" Audrey asked.

"Some churches are changing and are no longer as strict in their discipline, but my dad is bishop of our church ..." He paused. "I remember when I wanted to get my driver's license at age 16. Dad would not sign for me. He said he couldn't tell his church members to do one thing, and then make exceptions for his own family."

Audrey was quiet for several minutes. They were nearing Stevenson.

Back to safe subjects.

13

They were coming down the hill into the town. Johnny pointed out the courthouse, an imposing stone edifice on the square. There was the barber shop where he had his first haircut when he decided to be English. He'd bought new clothes at the department store and shaved off his beard and put on new clothes in the restroom of the courthouse basement. There was the hardware, where he had bought his bicycle, the one that he had ridden across the Southwest until it was smashed by that truck in Texas.

It occurred to him that she had seen all this before—the airport was on the other side of town and she had driven through here several times in the last ten days. Nevertheless, past history seemed a safe subject, and he told his stories.

They pulled up at the hitching rail of the courthouse. His business was inside.

"I'll just do some window shopping," she said. "When should I be back?"

"It shouldn't take more than half an hour."

When he emerged from the great stone edifice, back into the summer sunshine, Audrey was standing at Joyce's head, stroking the horse's nose and talking to her. Johnny noticed the shine of her hair, then looked quickly around. He was still acutely aware that he was an Amish man, accompanied by this striking, very *un-Amish* woman.

He untied Joyce as Audrey settled back into the seat with a sigh, and as they left Stevenson and headed toward home, she was quiet for the first few miles. He was glad not to have to force a conversation.

When she finally spoke, he was surprised to hear a distinct melancholy in her words.

"This week has been wonderful. I was so happy to be here for Naomi's wedding. She looked beautiful. I'm invited over to her house tomorrow, did you know that?" she asked him, but did not wait for an answer. "And that will be my last day here. It's time to get back to my own children, but I will be sad to leave here, too."

Johnny found himself ambushed by this; he had not been thinking about her leaving, but only about how her presence on his farm had changed his days.

"They'll be glad to see you … in Mexico …" he offered.

She grinned mischievously. "I hope so!"

And then she was silent again.

This was so unlike her that Johnny's relief at the suspension of conversation turned to an uncomfortable wondering about what Audrey might be thinking. Then, as Milford came into view again, she spoke, and every nerve in his brain and body flared up in alarm.

"I'm thinking about the last time we took a ride together," Audrey began. "My convertible. Up in the mountains. Along the ocean. So different from today."

Johnny remembered. With detailed clarity, he recalled the scene that had flashed through his mind that day, of him driving a red convertible, her auburn hair blowing in the wind, and three little children in the back seat. He had been shocked by the picture appearing, unbidden, in his mind.

That had happened when he thought he was looking for a new life. That was *before* the accident and *before* he made the decision to farm and come back home.

But the image had been etched in his memory—as was the guilt he had felt because of the immediate attraction that had drawn him to this woman. He was so unsettled by the memory that he barely noticed they were passing through the streets of Milford.

Now, he realized he was feeling the same attraction and the same guilt. Audrey had dominated his thoughts for days. This could not be. This was not the road he was meant to take.

Safe subjects.

"What happened to Sundancer?" he asked.

Sundancer was the race horse owned by Audrey's father. Samuel Cohraine had offered Johnny a job to help train the horse.

"He's doing very well, but he got tired of breathing Secretariat's dust. Daddy's already retired him." Sundancer had lost the Kentucky Derby by a nose to the mighty Secretariat.

"And what happened to you, Johnny?" Audrey asked.

There. It hung between them. She was not going to stay with safe subjects.

"When you left our house, I thought you were on a certain road," she went on. "Did the accident make you change your mind? Or did I just misunderstand? What changed your course?"

He shifted uncomfortably.

"There's something I need to explain," he began. "The time in the hospital …"

"You didn't remember anything. And I understood," she interrupted.

"But you were there. All that time. And my family was so thankful for your help."

She was silent, looking straight ahead, watching Joyce's ears flick back as though the horse were listening, too.

"I'm sorry that I didn't remember," said Johnny. "But I regret even more that I never called or wrote or thanked you in any way."

"Until today. You just did."

"But I really should have long before this. I just didn't know how or what to say."

"I'm glad you reached home safely. I prayed for you all that time, when we didn't know where you were or what was happening to you. I'm glad your mind and body healed well," she said brightly. "And I am so glad to be here for Naomi's wedding. I have loved every minute of this—experiencing the way you live. Your family has been so gracious, just opening their arms and welcoming me in. I'm the one who's grateful today."

He did not know how to say to her that she was the one who had made it easy. She had slipped into their everyday lives, *Almost,* he thought, *as though she belongs here.*

And then another image rose up in his vision: Audrey, in a long dress, with her auburn hair up under a white cap. Three little children peering out the back window of a buggy. Like the picture that had come to him one day long ago in California, this picture shook him.

Up ahead, he saw the school house. Their time together was almost over.

He heard his own voice, posing an unbelievable question.

"Do you think you could live this way? Be Amish?"

The green eyes left Joyce's ears and turned to Johnny's face.

She smiled at him, and he heard—what did he hear? He heard her tone before his brain interpreted her words. And what was in that tone? Regret? Sadness?

"Johnny," she lingered on his name. Her voice was softer and so low that he strained to hear every word over the rattling of the buggy wheels and the sound of Joyce's hooves on the pavement. "When I first met you … well, yes, I wanted to try. I was willing to do anything, because I thought … because … you know we had an instant connection. In just the very little time I knew you, I thought you might be the man I could spend a lifetime with. I didn't know then that you would choose to come back here, but if you would have asked me, I would have done it then. I wanted to try."

He was holding his breath.

"I thought this life was everything I wanted. The simplicity. The serenity. The community. And *you,*" she went on.

"But God seemed to have other plans for both of us. You came back here. I went to Mexico. I *know* that's where God wants me right now. I can't change the world, but I can change life for a few little people who need love and need to know that God cares about them."

Her eyes went back to the road.

"So whether or not I *could* live in your Amish world doesn't seem to be the question anymore. Although," she gently fingered a red spot on her right hand, "if I would have joined the Amish, you would have had to ask special permission for your wife to have an electric iron."

On down the road, Mandy was pulling a stack of envelopes and a newspaper from the mailbox. She saw the cart coming and lingered, waiting. When they were closer, she opened her mouth as though to say something, then, glancing at both faces, simply waved a greeting and turned quickly to go back to the house.

14

At breakfast the next morning, Audrey saw instantly that Johnny was upset. His mood had been so changeable during her visit that, when he appeared, she never knew whether to expect a cool, distant stranger or a jovial friend. His demeanor with her had changed slightly after their talk in the cemetery, but she knew their ride to Stevenson the day before would have shifted their relationship once again.

She had spent a restless night, reliving their conversation on the ride home. What else could she have said? What *should* she have said? She had spoken the truth, but her words, as she reviewed them, did not seem right. Had she been too flippant? Too cold? Too assuming? Too forward? Too blunt? Had she said enough? Not enough? What was Johnny thinking?

She wasn't sure what she expected from Johnny the next morning, but when the family gathered for breakfast, she was surprised yet again. His face was stern and his body tense, yet she somehow knew that she was not the cause. Something else was on his mind and had agitated him greatly.

Everyone caught his grim mood, and as soon as the prayer was finished, Johnny spoke, ignoring the food on the table before him.

"I had a letter from Annie's parents. It came earlier last week, but I didn't read it immediately. I should have … but I finally opened it last night."

"Not more bad news?" asked Mandy when Johnny paused.

"Yes. It seems that Joe, Annie's old boyfriend, has decided he wants to raise Christine as his daughter."

Audrey heard Mandy gasp.

"She *is* his daughter, isn't she?" asked John.

"Yes," Johnny's voice was hard, his words clipped. "But he wanted nothing to do with Annie and her baby. He treated Annie horribly and he abandoned them both. Why would he want a daughter now?"

"Maybe he is taking responsibility for the child, since her parents are now gone," suggested John.

"I doubt it," said Johnny sharply. "He was a hippie, into drugs and in jail several times. After Annie was here in Ohio, he tried to woo her back so that he could marry her and somehow avoid being drafted. I never met him, but everything I've heard about him doesn't lead me to think he's suddenly reformed and wanting to do the *responsible* thing."

"They cannot let him have her," said Mandy in a low voice. Audrey glanced at her. She was pale.

"Surely they won't?" asked Audrey. She was the outsider here; she knew nothing of this Joe, but she wanted to reassure and calm the apprehension she felt around the table.

"The family wouldn't do it; but he's threatened to hire a lawyer," answered Johnny, not looking at Audrey.

"How could he possibly have a claim on that little girl?" Audrey was beginning to feel anger rise in her own spirit.

"He *is* her father. I don't think anyone will contest that," said John.

"There has to be some way to stop this. They must stop it," said Mandy, her voice rising.

"It might not be in our hands," said John.

Johnny spoke up again. "Annie's parents wanted my advice, asked me if I could help in any way. They don't know what to do. But—" He spread his hands, palms upward, and shook his head slowly, "I don't know what to do. Especially if a lawyer gets involved."

"You need a good lawyer, too," said Audrey. "Dad. Call my dad. He'll advise you."

She saw immediately she had made a mistake. She wasn't sure what it was, but the three faces that turned toward her all told her that she had blundered.

"It would not be our way," said John quietly. "We do not use lawyers to settle our differences."

Audrey wanted to argue. She wanted to cry out, *But if this Joe is such a bad guy and he's hired an equally bad lawyer, Annie's parents don't stand a chance. You need a smart lawyer to fight this for you. You cannot just stand by and let it happen without a fight.*

But she remained silent, and her cheeks grew pink and warm. No one was paying attention to her discomfort, though.

"Besides," Johnny added, "we don't know for sure that he has a lawyer. It could just be a threat meant to bully them."

"The Lord will have to intervene," whispered Mandy. She had not touched the food on her plate. "He must! That man cannot have that little girl. Johnny, if only *you* were married, perhaps you could bring her here and raise her? Or Paul and Naomi? What about them? They could take her."

"I don't think either of those solutions would stop him, Mom. If Joe wants Christine, moving her to Ohio will not protect her."

The three sat in silence. Audrey fumed. They had to fight to protect the child! A little girl's life was at stake!

"Dad?" Johnny turned to his father. "I've always relied on you for wisdom. What can we do? What shall I tell the Yoders? They'll be waiting to hear from me."

John looked sad, Audrey thought. *And tired.*

"I don't know, son. This is something so far from our experience … I will write to their bishop, and we'll see if he knows more about the situation and has any ideas of what could be done. Perhaps we are jumping to conclusions. Perhaps the man has had a miraculous change of heart. Perhaps this is truly God's will for Christine, and it will turn out for her good. Let me see what more I can learn."

"But until letters go back and forth, it could be too late!" The words burst from Audrey's lips. She couldn't hold them back.

John looked at her. "It is truly in God's hands, as are all things. We might be His instruments in this situation, but His plan will prevail."

***

No one ate much. After the devotions—which, Audrey thought, no one seemed to hear—they all rose from their chairs and silently went to their tasks for the morning.

Audrey carried plates and cups to the kitchen sink. Mandy was standing at the window, staring at the garden. Audrey saw the streak of a tear on one cheek.

"Mandy," she said, gently touching the older woman's arm. "Who is this Joe? Why is the thought of Christine's father raising her such a terrible thing?"

Mandy turned tear-filled eyes toward Audrey.

"I cannot tell you, dear. It is not my secret to tell. All I can tell you is that he is not a good man. And if I could, I'd whisk that child up and take her away, somewhere that man would never find her."

15

Audrey left for Naomi's house as soon as the dishes were put away. Johnny went about his chores with little thought about what he was doing. His mind was in Indiana, in the Yoder home, where a little girl was probably playing in the sunshine with no idea of the danger circling around her. She was *Annie's* little girl.

Annie's last words to him had been about Christine. In the letter she had written to Johnny the night before she died and as she stood with him at the gates of Heaven, she had said Christine would need him. Could Annie have known this was going to happen? How was that possible? Yet, her words had been very clear, and Johnny understood that Annie was telling him he must, in some way, provide for Christine.

But this! He was helpless to know what was to be done in this situation. How could the little girl be protected? What could he, an Amish farmer, do about Joe's threat? Johnny had been Annie's husband, but he had never been Christine's father. Annie had given birth to her daughter when she was very young, and the baby was given to Henry and Betty to raise as their own.

What right did Johnny have to meddle in this? But he could not stand by and let this happen! This was Annie's daughter, and he was still considered a son in the Yoder household.

In the end, the one thing that convinced him he had some sort of responsibility to Christine was the memory of Annie's last words—repeated twice. Somehow, Annie had known.

His head was spinning as he sank into Annie's chair late in the evening, exhausted from the debates that had gone on inside his head all day. He did not remember exactly what he'd done that day in the barn; he did not even try to remember. He only knew that he was no further along in finding an answer concerning Christine than he had been in the morning.

The house was growing darker. He had not yet lit the lamps.

He heard a soft knock on the kitchen door. No one ever knocked. He rose from the chair and opened the door.

Audrey stood there in the twilight. She had been gone all day, visiting Naomi in her new home—Paul and Naomi's home.

"Audrey ..." he stepped back, making way for her to enter his house. The thought flashed through his mind that in all the time she'd been on the farm she had never come into his house.

It appeared that she would not tonight, either. She did not move, but stood outside.

"Johnny, I've been thinking all day. I know that it's not your way to make use of lawyers and the courts," she was talking softly but firmly, seeming to be afraid to cross a boundary again and yet certain of what she wanted to say. "But I stopped in town today before I went to Naomi's, and I called Dad. I feel so strongly that you've *got* to find out where this matter of Christine stands legally. Maybe Joe doesn't have a chance at all, and so there's no need for everyone to be so worried about him. Or maybe he does have a reasonable case, and then you will have to have a plan. This is Annie's child, Johnny!"

He was surprised at the passion in her voice. She was defending Annie's child. And she had never known Annie or Christine. She went on, not waiting for an answer, and her pleading cut deep. He felt as though an old wound inside him was being ripped open.

"Please, please, talk to Dad. Just ask for his advice. He may be able to help you without your hiring a lawyer or going to court. Please, Johnny, just talk to him. See what he thinks."

"You've already spoken with him?"

"Yes. I apologize if you think it was wrong of me to do so, but I had to talk to him. He's willing to discuss the situation with you. Give him a call tonight. He promised he'd be home. I told him you'd have to go to the pay phone, but he said to call collect. Please, Johnny. Just get an idea of what he thinks."

"Tonight yet?"

"Yes. It's only a little after six out there. He's waiting."

She held out a small piece of paper.

"Here's the number. Please. Please."

He took it from her fingers and his eyes met hers.

"All right. I'll call him."

The evening was shadowy, and he couldn't be sure—but he thought she was going to throw her arms around him. She caught herself, though, quietly said, "Thank you," and turned back to the big house.

He watched her go. She did not look back.

Then he turned to get a lantern.

* * *

The telephone rang twice, three times, four times. After the fifth ring, a strong, authoritative voice answered. He recognized Samuel Cohraine's take-charge tone.

"Mr. Cohraine, this is Johnny Miller," he began, but Samuel did not wait for long preambles. He interrupted.

"Young man, good to hear from you. Audrey tells me you've got some trouble brewing."

"Yes, sir, well, we think so."

"First, let's get something else out of the way. I want you to know that my job offer still stands. I still want you working for me. Remember that."

"Yes, sir, and I appreciate the offer, but I'm back in Ohio and farming now."

"Yes, yes, but a man sometimes changes his mind or needs a little adventure. Just keep me in mind."

Johnny wanted to move on to the problem at hand, but when he started to explain, it seemed Samuel already knew as many details as the Millers did.

"Is there money involved somewhere, Johnny?" Samuel asked.

"What?" asked Johnny, not quite understanding what the lawyer was asking.

"It's always about the money," said Samuel. "The man's after a windfall, I'll bet on it. Can he gain financially by claiming the girl?"

"I … I don't know," Johnny said. This was a new thought for him. "Christine's parents had a large farm; they were doing well, as far as I know."

"And she is the only survivor, right? And the car that crashed into the buggy was driven by someone who was drunk and will also have to cough up some money. He's after the money, Johnny."

"Is there anything we can do to stop him?"

"There's always *something* you can do. Some courses of action are not as ethical as others. We need to know a little more about this Joe character. With my resources, I should be able to help you. I've got connections in Indianapolis. Let me find an attorney in that area who would handle family matters like that."

No, no, we do not want to go down this path, thought Johnny.

"Mr. Cohraine, we don't want to involve lawyers. Audrey simply suggested that you might have some ideas for us."

"I understand, Johnny." *Did he, really?* "But we do need to find out a few things about who we're dealing with. I'll not make any promises for you or commit to anything; I'll just get you more information. Will that do?"

"I suppose," said Johnny, although he wasn't sure exactly what the lawyer was proposing.

"I'll call you tomorrow from the office."

"No, you can't call me. I'll have to call you."

"Oh, that's right. Say, three o'clock?"

Johnny thanked the lawyer again, and hung up.

Somehow the conversation had not gone as planned; Samuel Cohraine, as usual, had driven things his own way. Johnny tried to sort out his thoughts and feelings, but the only thing he was certain of was that he felt turmoil and sadness.

16

Johnny and his father were almost finished with the milking the next morning when Audrey appeared in the doorway. Johnny saw immediately that she had on the same outfit she had worn the day she first appeared so unexpectedly in the barn. She was dressed for travel. Her time at the Miller farm was at an end.

He had been so preoccupied with the news of Christine's danger the day before that he had not thought about this moment. She was leaving. She would probably never be back here. He would never see her again. Instead of relief, he suddenly felt like a man stranded on a deserted island, watching a ship go by, unaware of his plight. There were still things to talk about, still things he needed to sort out—

Audrey solemnly shook hands with both men and thanked them for their hospitality. John turned away, then, leaving the two younger people to say goodbye.

Her eyes met his, and she smiled.

"Goodbye, Johnny. Thank you for calling Dad last night. And when you and Joyce feel like an outing, come see the butterflies." He thought that the sadness in her eyes was lit, for a brief moment, by a flicker of mischief. "But please, don't even think of bringing a bicycle."

Before he could say anything, she turned away and was gone.

***

That evening at the supper table, Johnny reported on his afternoon conversation with the California lawyer. Cohraine had taken his call promptly at three o'clock, even though he had a client waiting outside his office.

"Mr. Cohraine gave me the name and number of a lawyer," Johnny began.

"We will not go through the courts," said John firmly.

"I know. I tried to explain that to him, but I think it's impossible for him to think of settling anything without an attorney being involved," answered Johnny. "He gave me the name of a lawyer and said that this man would 'get us the child' if we don't care about his tactics. There are ways, apparently, to make Joe back off, including creating trouble for *him*."

"That sounds awful," said Mandy.

John nodded at his wife. "It probably is. We will not ask for this man's help."

"This lawyer in Indianapolis will get us more information, if we want it," offered Johnny, but as soon as the words were out of his mouth, he regretted them. He was actually thinking of doing business with a man whose "tactics" might be less than upright!

"I sent off a letter to the Yoders' bishop today," said John. "But maybe it would be better if I went out to Indiana instead of waiting for an answer. Audrey might be right in that. We might not have time to waste."

"No," said Johnny. "If anyone goes, it should be me. I don't have any idea what my presence there might accomplish, but at least I can talk with the Yoders and maybe I will learn more.

"There's only one thing," he went on. "Audrey's father—Mr. Cohraine—was very firm. He said we should have *no* communication with Joe."

"He won't even know you're there, will he?" asked Mandy. "He doesn't know you; you don't know him. I can't see that a visit to the Yoders would be a problem."

"But if our paths should just happen to cross, do you think, Dad, that I should try to talk with him?"

"Hold on a minute," said John. "We're jumping to conclusions. We don't even know if Joe lives in the area. We don't know what kind of man he is now; we're only going on what we heard about him in the past. Son, why don't you first call the Yoders and find out if there have been any developments since they sent you that letter. Then make the suggestion that you come for a visit. See what they have to say before you make the trip out there."

That seemed a sensible plan, and after supper, Johnny walked down to the telephone booth with a handful of change.

* * *

The hay would soon be ready to cut, and the field down along the creek still must be planted in corn. The spring had been unusually wet, and some farmers who had planted early were actually now replanting fields after their first seeding had been overwhelmed by floods. Johnny had watched that one field closely and decided to wait to plant. He would take a chance on a late corn-picking rather than have to plant two or even three times. But timing was always crucial when deciding when to get the hay in, too. The hay must come first, then the corn could be planted.

It was not a good time to leave the farm, Johnny told himself as he walked through the field, the tall alfalfa brushing his legs. And even if he did go to Indiana, what could he possibly accomplish?

He had been unable to contact the Yoders the night before. When Annie was alive, she would sometimes call her parents' neighbors, who were English and had a phone. The neighbors would take a message to Annie's parents.

Johnny had tried that approach. There was no answer at the neighbors' house. He had tried early the next morning, hoping to catch them before they left the house. Still no answer. They must be away. There was no way to contact the Yoders, other than by sending a letter.

"A letter will take days," he lamented to John and Mandy at lunch.

"And another few days for their answer to get back to us," Mandy added.

"I would advise, son, that you get there as quickly as you can. Call a driver. Go. Who knows what is happening out there?" said John.

Johnny stared at his coffee cup, thinking about his fields and the weather.

He heard Annie's words, *Christine will need you.*

"I'll see that the work gets done. Paul might be able to help out, and I'll hire someone, if necessary," offered John.

"All right. I'll call a driver and go first thing tomorrow."

"Son, I know this may not be a good time, but if you're headed to Indiana anyway, do you think you should also go up to Nappanee and see Orin Borntrager?"

Orin Borntrager? Who was that?

"He's still waiting on an answer from me about you meeting that widow," said John.

Oh.

"Dad, I really don't think this is a good time to make any big decisions like that."

***

At the telephone booth once again, Johnny scanned the list taped to the glass wall. The Millers had their preferred drivers, of course—every Amish family did. In addition, the wall was almost covered with cards of businesses or scrawled notes with phone numbers placed there by English people willing to hire out their time and car to taxi the horse-and-buggy folks. This wall was, in essence, the local phone directory.

He dialed the first number.

Fifteen minutes later, he had tried almost every number on the list and was almost out of coins to feed into the phone. Tomorrow would be Friday, and many drivers were already booked for weekly trips to town or they didn't want to be making a long trip going into the weekend. One or two were interested until Johnny told them he was not certain when he would return. Then they politely declined.

Almost convinced he would have to wait until Monday to leave, he ruffled through the cards and papers hanging on the glass wall. Was there someone he had forgotten?

He caught a glimpse of a bright blue business card tucked behind three layers of miscellaneous scraps of paper. Only a corner showed. He moved the other papers gently and pulled out the card.

The words on it said simply, DRIVING. CALL MIKE. Below was a number Johnny did not recognize.

"Hello?" a deep, strong voice answered on the second ring.

"Are you Mike? I'm looking for a driver to go to Indiana early tomorrow morning. I don't know when I'll be returning, but I found your card and wondered if you're available tomorrow?"

"Sure am. What's the name and address? And how many of you will there be?"

Johnny gave him the information, and they agreed that Mike would be at the Miller farm at 6 a.m. the next morning. Johnny did hope that he could make the trip out to the Yoders' home, talk with them, and return home in the evening. The earlier they started, the sooner he'd be home.

Relieved, he carefully positioned the bright blue card back on the wall—this time, on top of the layers of notes, in plain sight.

17

Mike arrived at two minutes before six the next morning. Johnny had packed an overnight bag, just in case his visit would have to be extended. He put his bag in the back seat and noticed that Mike also had a small bag. He also took note of how clean the car was—from shiny wheels to spotless carpets and sparkling windows, the car looked well cared for and almost new. The car had not recently been traveling on the country gravel roads. Or else Mike washed and cleaned it every day.

The deep, strong voice on the phone had given Johnny the expectation of a big, burly man. Mike was big—in the vertical sense. Even though he remained in his seat while Johnny climbed into the car, Johnny judged the driver to be almost a head taller than he was. But he was a stringbean of a man, as Mandy would have said. His shirt hung loosely, looking three sizes too large for his body, and his arms seemed to be only bones covered with skin—there was no sign of muscle. The car was a larger model, but even so, Mike's skinny knees constantly banged up against the steering wheel. And he was older than Johnny had expected—at least 65, maybe close to 70. His hair was pure white.

They introduced themselves as Mike swung the car out of the driveway and turned toward Milford.

"So. Indiana?"

"Yes," Johnny said.

"You have an address?"

"Not really. I can get you there, though."

"Good enough for me," replied Mike easily.

Johnny soon discovered that Mike hummed while he drove. There appeared to be a radio in the car, but Mike never glanced at the dial. He just hummed quietly to himself.

Except when they were talking, and Johnny also soon discovered that Mike was quite a talkative person once he got started. Or, more accurately, he was curious. Johnny realized that Mike was not talking about himself—he wanted to know more about Johnny.

"So. Headed out for business?"

"No. We have a family situation that I need to check into."

"So. Family. I hope it's not a serious emergency?"

"It could be. We don't know yet. That's why I'm going." Johnny didn't really mind that Mike was so inquisitive. Actually, he welcomed a chance to talk with someone outside the situation—perhaps it would help him sort out his thoughts. He heard his own answers to Mike's questions and knew that he sounded evasive. But it was just that he didn't know where to start.

Mike was humming to himself.

"My wife has … had … a daughter. She's six. She was being raised by my wife's sister and brother-in-law, but they were killed in a buggy accident. Now there seems to be a question about who should raise the little girl."

Mike didn't take his eyes off the road, but Johnny felt the next question bore into him.

"Your wife isn't going to raise her?"

"My wife died a year and a half ago," he said quietly.

"Oh, I'm sorry," said Mike, his two silver eyebrows drawing together.

"It's a long and complicated story," Johnny said. "And I'm afraid that Christine's—that's the little girl—that her life is going to be determined by what may or may not happen. Christine's father, who was my wife's boyfriend before we met, is trying to lay claim to her now. He never cared about her and has never even seen her, as far as I know. Annie—my wife—and he went their separate ways when Annie found out she was expecting a baby."

Mike stopped humming and shook his head.

"Unfortunately, as far as we know, this Joe, Christine's father, is an unsavory character. Christine's with her grandparents now, and they've asked me for help and advice. I don't know what can be done, but I thought I'd visit them and see how things stand."

"So. Sounds like you need a good attorney," Mike said.

"We choose not to use that alternative," answered Johnny. "There has to be a better way to work things out."

"I agree." Mike nodded solemnly. "There has to be a better way than what we're doing to each other in the courts these days."

***

The morning and the miles rolled by. Johnny found himself liking Mike more and more as they talked. It did not escape his attention, though, that most of their talk was about Johnny and his life—while Mike was learning a great deal about Johnny, Johnny was discovering very little about Mike.

They stopped once, at a small restaurant along the highway. Mike needed a break and wanted a cup of coffee. He unfolded his long frame from the car seat and then took a moment to slowly straighten up, as though his body needed time to remember how to walk.

"Getting to the place that I stiffen up if I sit too long," he said as he stretched a bit more, then started toward the door of the diner.

Johnny followed, two steps behind the tall figure, and he noticed that Mike walked with a distinct limp.

Soon after the coffee stop, a sign welcomed them to Indiana and reminded Johnny of the first time he had traveled with Annie to her home. That had also been the first time he had been outside the state of Ohio. As he reminisced, he found himself giving Mike a condensed history of the last five years of his life—the story of how he and Annie had met, how Annie had loved Monarch butterflies and compared their transformation to the transformation Jesus could bring to a life—"a worm to a butterfly," she had often said. He reflected on how Jesus had changed his own life, and the devastation that followed Annie's death. His memories carried him across the country, as he set out on an old bicycle to pedal his way to a new life. He had met Wandering Willie, and Audrey (here, he paused for a moment before going on, and out of the corner of his eye, he caught Mike glancing at him) and her father Samuel, Big Bill McCollum, and the people at the commune, Sydney and Lisa.

Mike laughed heartily as Johnny described how Sydney's popular new designs were inspired by Johnny's barn-door pants.

"So. You are now a fashion plate, eh?" he joked, raising one silver eyebrow in Johnny's direction.

"Hardly," Johnny shot back. "It's difficult to imagine that Hollywood stars and big-city people would adopt our simple clothes as the latest style. But ..."

He paused. Mike waited.

"But apparently, they have. I contributed $20 to Sydney to help him get a start in business, and now he's been sending me checks every month. And they aren't small checks, either. Apparently, the West Coast is going wild over Johnny BarnDoors."

Mike laughed.

"So. You're getting rich!"

"To tell you the truth, I'm not sure how I feel about this money. I only intended to help Sydney get started, but now it seems as though ..."

He didn't quite know how to explain it.

"As though you're making money from selling off bits of your Amish lifestyle." Mike voiced the thought for him.

"Yes. I'm not sure I *like* this income stream, strange as that may sound."

"Not strange at all," replied Mike. "But have you ever considered that maybe this is not about you getting rich? Maybe this is happening because of something going on in Sydney's life, and you are a beneficiary, paid back for your kindness. Or maybe the money is being given to you for another reason."

Now Johnny felt even more unease. An idea had been lurking in the corners of his mind. He had refused to usher in the unwelcome thought and give it the time of day. But it was there, waiting for him to give it consideration. And Mike had just pushed Johnny toward opening the door.

Johnny looked at Mike, measuring the man and their developing friendship. *Oh, what could it hurt to tell him?*

"I've got my checkbook along. My friend Samuel, who is an attorney, says it's always about money."

Mike considered this.

He doesn't seem shocked, thought Johnny.

"So. You think you might be able to buy him off?"

"If this entire situation has come about only because Joe is looking to gain financially, then I am pretty certain I *can* buy him off, as you put it. I could even promise him more to come. The question is, should I? Do I want to?"

"Does it feel like blackmail?" asked Mike.

"More like I'm buying a person," answered Johnny soberly. "That thought almost makes me sick. But if it will save Christine, then ..."

"Then is it right?" Mike finished again.

"Yes. Would it be all right, if, by doing it, we can save a person?"

"So. A dilemma for you," Mike said, tilting his head. "That old question—does the end justify the means?"

"Is there no other way? There has to be another way," said Johnny, more to himself than to his new friend.

"Divine intervention, maybe," replied Mike. "All I will say, my friend, is that there is no such thing as coincidence. God has His purposes in everything."

***

The thought occurred to Johnny that this stranger would soon know everything about his life. And for some reason, Johnny felt quite comfortable with that. The two had somehow made a connection as friends, and Johnny felt his confidences—even about these thoughts that were troubling him—were safe with Mike.

As a matter of fact, the tall, skinny, white-haired driver reminded him of someone. The minute Johnny had got into the car that morning, this stranger had seemed … not a stranger. Johnny couldn't quite explain it, but he felt as though he had known Mike for a long time, maybe even all of his life. Johnny wondered if perhaps Mike had been Amish years ago, when Johnny was still a boy, and now, being English and years older, looked quite different than Johnny would have remembered. Or could Mike be someone Johnny had met briefly in his travels across the country? That would be quite a coincidence. Yet the feeling persisted that they had met before.

At one point, Johnny tried to find out more about his new friend.

"Have we met before? It almost feels as though we have, but I'm sorry, I can't remember it if we did," Johnny began.

"I don't think so," returned Mike. "But I'm an average sort of guy. Probably lots of people walking around that look like me."

"I've been thinking about it and wondering if maybe—and this would be amazing—but maybe I met you somewhere out west? On the bus? In a restaurant somewhere? Maybe before I had my bicycle accident. I did lose my memory temporarily then, and maybe that's why I can't remember. Where are you from?"

"Oh, I've lived and worked here and there," replied Mike. "So. You lost your memory? What must that have been like?"

And just like that, they were back to Johnny telling his story and Mike listening to every word.

18

When Mrs. Yoder opened the door and found Johnny on her porch, tears immediately filled her eyes. Mike declined her invitation to also come into the house; he would sit in one of the comfortable Adirondacks on the porch and perhaps take a nap, he said.

Annie's father worked away, at a factory in town. Johnny had forgotten to take that into consideration when he planned his visit to the Yoders' home. So it was only Johnny and Mrs. Yoder who sat down at the kitchen table. She made them both a cup of coffee and brought out an apple pie.

"We have been waiting to hear from you, but we didn't expect to see you here. At least, not so soon."

"We didn't know how urgent the situation was," Johnny replied. "So I thought I'd come and find out, firsthand."

He also realized that Christine was not in the house. Mrs. Yoder explained that she was playing at the neighbors' home, a short way down the road. It was just as well. He remembered how much the child looked like her mother, and he did not think he wanted to see her today.

"Do we know what Joe's up to?" he asked.

"We have had only the one letter." Mrs. Yoder rose, went to a small desk in the corner, and took a long envelope from one cubbyhole. She handed it to Johnny.

The address was written in a large, uneven hand, and there was no return address. Pulling out the single sheet of paper, Johnny quickly read the contents. This, too, was handwritten, probably by Joe, and with very poor spelling and punctuation. The lack of refinement in the appearance of the letter only added to the ugliness of the threat: Christine was Joe's daughter and he was going to legally claim her. He had every right to do this, and if they did not give her to him, they would be hearing from his attorney.

In his imagination, Johnny could hear Mike comment on this: "So. He doesn't have a lawyer yet."

Joe was trying to bully them into turning the child over to him. But the question was—if they refused to buckle under his bluff, would he really have any legal right?

Mike had dropped that casual statement: God has a purpose in everything. What purpose could there possibly be in this situation?

"You haven't responded to him?"

"No," Mrs. Yoder shook her head, and Johnny saw some of the fire in her eyes that Annie had talked about—back in the days of Annie's rebellious youth, her mother had been a sharp, critical woman, but she had changed in the last few years. Still, Johnny could see that she would not bow to Joe without a fight. "No, we don't have an address for him. We don't even know where he lives. There are rumors that he's back in the area again and lives somewhere out in the sticks, all by himself, but we have no way to contact him."

"And this letter is to put fear into you. I suppose he will give you time to worry, and then he'll contact you again."

Mrs. Yoder frowned slightly. "He's always been trouble. His mother spoiled him. He seemed to disappear for a while after Annie turned him down the last time, but people have seen him around again. We don't know where he's living or if he's working. Nobody has anything good to say about him. When this letter turned up—" She hunched her shoulders as though cold. "I can almost feel the evil when I think about things he's done. Do you suppose he knows where Christine is?"

"Of course he does," Johnny answered. "He had your address to send this letter. And it's obvious he knows that Christine is with you."

Her eyes widened, as though she had not realized this.

"He wouldn't … he wouldn't actually try to *steal her*—would he?" Her voice was little more than a whisper.

"I don't know the man. But I'd certainly hope he wouldn't do anything like that. I think, judging from this letter, that he believes he can scare you into doing what he wants."

"Why? Why is he suddenly interested in Christine?"

"It's possible that he's interested in financial gain. Maybe he thinks, as the only survivor, Christine is now in possession of a lot of money. Maybe he wants to claim Henry and Betty's farm and sell it."

"Oh," said Mrs. Yoder quietly. "Well, what can we do? What shall we do?"

He heard the edge of fear in her voice.

"I don't know. I just don't know," he replied. "From the looks of this letter, he doesn't have an attorney—at least, not yet—or the letter would have come from the lawyer. He hasn't given you any way of contacting him or answering him. And yet, I'm convinced that he's not bluffing, and he won't drop this and disappear if you ignore him. He's just waiting … for something."

Christine's grandmother gave a deep sigh.

"I have a friend," Johnny started, "who is an attorney."

Mrs. Yoder looked up at him, her eyes full of skepticism.

"No, I don't intend to take this to court, but maybe Samuel can at least advise us on whether or not it's even possible that Joe could get Christine." He did not add that the last time he had talked to Samuel, the attorney had seemed to be deaf to his staunch stand against using legal action.

"All right," Annie's mother said with resignation. "We will do nothing for now. But, of course, we wouldn't know what to do anyway. Dad will be home by 3:30. Will you wait until he is here, and talk with him?"

"I have some other business in the area," Johnny heard himself answer, but he wondered why he had said that. He had planned to talk with the Yoders and then turn around and go home. "And I wanted to get back home tonight. But I'll see. If I can, I'll stop back before leaving."

***

"Something strange happened in there," Johnny told Mike as they drove away from the Yoders' home.

Mike said nothing, just lifted an inquiring eyebrow.

"Mom Yoder asked me to stay until Annie's dad got home. But I heard myself say—no, it was almost as though someone else was talking for me—I said I had other business in town. Why did I say that? I have no other plans here."

"Hmm," said Mike. "So?"

"So what?"

"So which way are we going now?"

Johnny gave an exasperated sound. "I don't know. I was planning on going home. There's nothing I can do here."

"Did you get any more information?"

"Not much more than what we already knew. Except that he probably doesn't have an attorney. At least, not yet."

"That might be good news."

"Mike, you said something earlier about divine intervention. I believe God cares about everything that happens in our lives. I believe He does intervene. It's just that sometimes—sometimes it's hard to *see* that or *feel* it. But I believe that's true. I also believe in prayer. And I've been praying for wisdom."

Mike was driving and listening. Not humming. Not commenting. Just waiting for Johnny.

"I've been praying for wisdom. And now I feel as if I *do* have something more to do here."

"So …?" Mike again raised that one inquiring silver eyebrow in Johnny's direction.

Johnny took a deep breath.

"I think I should talk with Joe."

Now Mike did take his eyes off the road. He looked at Johnny with a faint smile.

"Do you think that's a prompt from God? An answer to your prayer for wisdom?"

Johnny couldn't tell if he was mocking him or gently approving.

"I'm not sure. I'm not at all sure. But I feel I have to do it. I don't know what I'd say to him. I don't even know where to find him. I just feel this compulsion to at least try to contact him."

"Well, there's a diner up ahead. In my travels, I've found that's usually a good place to get information about the neighborhood. Let's give it a try. Besides, I'm hungry."

And with that, their course was set.

* * *

The sign over the door said MABEL'S, but Johnny noticed that the cook in the back was a short, balding man with a round, red face. Certainly not Mabel.

Only half the chairs in the diner were full. It was the middle of the afternoon, and some patrons seemed to be lingering after a late lunch while others had apparently stopped in for a cup of coffee or an afternoon pastry.

Mike's complaint that he was hungry reminded Johnny that they had not had lunch. Mrs. Yoder had served him pie and coffee, but Mike had not had anything to eat since breakfast, at least, nothing that Johnny knew of. Johnny suddenly felt the need for meat and potatoes. He ordered a ham dinner, and Mike chose a beef stew. Johnny was surprised at how hungry he was, even after eating a large piece of pie less than an hour before.

The waitress was a young lady who could not have been more than 19. Her curly hair was cut short, in a boyish style. She smiled constantly and her laughter often rippled above the low hum of conversation and the sounds of pots and pans in the kitchen. She was genuinely enjoying her customers. Her name tag said *Ellie*.

When she stopped to refill their coffee cups, Johnny asked her, "Do you know a Joe Byler who lives around here?"

She took a moment to think.

"No. I don't think I do. Even though that's a pretty common name—there could be six men in this community with that name, but I don't know any of them."

She went on. "But Hank over there … he knows everybody around here. And when someone new moves in, he's one of the first ones to get to know them. Check with him. He might know the man you're looking for."

Hank, a muscular, dark-haired man in his thirties, was seated in a booth, talking with a young man. The young man's face was pale, with sharp creases in his forehead. A book lay between them, and Hank was making notes on a sheet of paper. Their conversation seemed so intense and earnest that Johnny hesitated to interrupt. But he did.

"Excuse me. The waitress said you might know where we could find a Joe Byler."

Hank's moustache twitched slightly. Johnny thought that the man had started to say something and then thought better of it.

"Would it be Cheese Henry's Joe you're looking for?"

"I don't really know. I've never met the man. He would be about my age. As far as I know, he's not married. The last I heard of him, he looked like a hippie and rode a motorcycle."

The moustache twitched again; this time, Johnny was certain of it.

"That would probably be Cheese Henry's Joe. Is he expecting you?"

"No, but we need to see him … on a very important issue."

The man pulled a small notepad from his shirt pocket and picked up his pen lying on the table.

"Best I can do is draw you a map. I don't think the address alone will get you there."

"Thanks. I would appreciate it."

Johnny watched the squiggles and arrows take shape on the paper. At a few intersections, Hank carefully noted road numbers.

"Tell you the truth, I'm not even sure the road signs are there. We locals just pretty much know the roads without having to look for signs."

"I understand," Johnny said. "That sounds like home."

"Where is home?"

"Milford, Ohio."

"Well, good luck with this," Hank said, handing the slip of paper to Johnny. "And good luck with Joe. He's pretty much of a recluse. But I hope you get what you came all this way for."

19

"Well, I didn't plan on this," said Johnny as they walked out to the car. He noticed that he had been unconsciously slowing his pace to match Mike's lopsided gait.

The older man grinned at him across the roof of the car as they both opened their doors.

"So. We never know what a day has in store."

Johnny paused for a moment and looked at the flat countryside. The diner was close to the highway, inviting hungry travelers to stop in. Across the parking lot, a tired-looking motel faced the diner with its long row of bright blue doors. Even at a distance, Johnny could see the spots where the bright blue had peeled off. As if to compensate, small flower boxes were placed at intervals along the sidewalk, planted with straggly blue and white flowers that were struggling to survive. Other than those two businesses, the view for miles around was of large farm fields, broken only by clusters of farm buildings with a few trees huddling around the houses. A person could see for miles out here.

Yes, he thought. *Mike's right. Life is much more like the hills and valleys back home—we never know what is around the bend or over the next hill.*

He settled into his seat next to Mike and studied the map Hank had drawn on the small paper.

"I have no idea which way we're going. The first landmark we're looking for is a T-road ... I think." He handed the paper to Mike.

Mike looked at the paper, gave it a turn clockwise, tilted his head and peered at it, gave it another turn, then handed it back to Johnny.

"We'll find him somehow."

And then what? Johnny had no idea what he would say to this man from Annie's past who had created so much heartache years ago and had now reappeared to stir up trouble again. The uncertainty was unsettling to Johnny. He liked to have a plan. He liked to be in control. He liked to know where he was going. *But life wasn't like that, was it?*

"Wait a minute," he said suddenly as Mike turned the ignition. "I want to make a call."

Mike shut off the car again without a word. Johnny dug into his wallet and found what he was looking for—a white card.

"Shouldn't take long," he said to Mike.

Stepping back inside the diner, he looked around the perimeter of the room. A short hallway led off the main dining area, and hanging on the wall in the hallway was a pay phone.

Johnny laid the business card on the phone's small shelf and dialed Samuel Cohraine's office number.

When the receptionist answered, he had to smile. Every time he heard her voice, he was reminded of that first day he had walked into Cohraine's plush law office and the lady behind the desk had given him one look and decided he was a vagrant who had wandered in off the street on some nefarious mission.

The attorney was not in, the woman stated crisply. He would not return until Monday morning.

Johnny thanked her, hung up, and tried Samuel's home number. He wondered if Audrey was in California.

Samuel answered the phone.

"Mr. Cohraine, it's Johnny Miller."

"Johnny! How are you doing? What's happening?"

"I'm calling for some advice." Johnny decided to get right to the point. "I'm in Indiana. Someone has told me where to find Joe. I think I'm going to try to talk to him, see if he can be talked out of whatever it is he's planning." He wasn't sure what he was saying, or what he wanted to say. "I don't know exactly what I'm doing or hope to do. I came out here, intending to talk to Annie's parents about the situation, but somehow I'm now on Joe's trail."

"No, Johnny, absolutely do not talk with the man. Stay away from him. Let an attorney deal with it."

"But I've seen the letter he sent to the Yoders. He wrote it himself. I don't believe he has an attorney. At least, not yet. I think at this point he is trying to bully them into doing what he says. Maybe we can stop this thing before it even gets to an attorney or the courts."

"Look, Johnny," said Samuel. "I know you don't want to involve lawyers, but I did some checking on my own. This guy's a sleazeball. He's had jail time. It appears that he left the country and went to Canada to evade the draft. And then there's the circumstances of the car crash that killed Christine's parents. The driver was drunk, and he's a man very well-off and very well-known in that town. I tell you, Joe's intention is to sue the driver. He'll claim Christine as his daughter and ask for a big settlement. I don't know yet what kind of estate Christine will inherit, but you can bet that he wants to get his hands on that, too. Stay away from him, Johnny. You won't achieve anything by trying to talk to the guy. Money's talking to him right now, and money talks much louder than anything you could say to him."

Johnny was silent, listening, trying to decide how to answer Samuel. Samuel was talking *facts*. But there was something else that had to be considered. Johnny couldn't put his finger on exactly what it was ... but he knew there was *something else*.

"There are other ways of handling this," Samuel went on. "I have the name of an attorney who could—well, he could arrange things for you. I couldn't do what he does, but he gets results. He can probably get this character to back off. And let's face it, Joe's going to have a hard time in court. He's got a record. He's a draft dodger. We don't know if he has any way to support a daughter. I have to say, I'm surprised that he's even considering taking this to court."

"Maybe he's not," interrupted Johnny. It was difficult to get a word in edgewise with Samuel Cohraine. "Maybe he's hoping to scare the Yoders into doing what he says."

"But there's one more thing that's going to work against him. As a matter of fact, I don't think he has a leg to stand on. Have you seen Christine's birth certificate, Johnny?" asked Cohraine.

"No," said Johnny. "What difference would that make?"

"In this case, quite a bit of difference. His name isn't on—"

"I'm sorry, your three minutes are up."

The automated signal broke into Cohraine's sentence and asked for more money to continue the conversation. Johnny fished in his pocket for more coins and found only a nickel and six pennies.

The line went dead.

Johnny hurried back to the cashier's station. Two middle-aged ladies were standing there with checks in hand, chatting with Ellie. Apparently Ellie had a new boyfriend, and the two women wanted all the details on the new romance. Ellie's cheeks were pink; and from her flustered giggles, Johnny could tell that she wasn't thinking about customers at the moment. He stood behind the two women, his wallet in his hand, trying to be patient.

Finally, one of the women noticed him and gave a small laugh.

"Oh, here we are, holding up your line, Ellie. Well, you'll just have to fill us in later," she said and handed her check to the young waitress.

Ellie looked relieved and gave the woman her change. Then the next lady also had a bill to pay and a few more words of advice on romance to pass on to Ellie.

At last, Johnny was in front of the register. He handed Ellie a five-dollar bill.

"Could I have change, please? In quarters?"

Ellie punched a key and the drawer slid open. Three quarters lay in one slot.

"I'll have to go in the back and get another roll," she said. And before Johnny could reply, she slipped away from the register.

Eventually he returned to the pay phone with a handful of coins. But when he dialed Cohraine's number again, Mrs. Cohraine's voice answered. She was apologetic. Samuel had had to leave. Could Johnny call back later in the evening?

Johnny told her he wasn't sure, thanked her, and said goodbye.

What was Samuel going to say? Something about Joe's name ... not on the birth certificate? Is that what he was going to say? But why wouldn't Joe's name be there? He was Christine's father. No one had ever questioned that.

Johnny stood there a moment, wondering what his next step should be. Samuel had been so emphatic. He should *not, definitely not* try to talk with Joe. Well, then, what was there to do? He knew he was *not, definitely not* going to talk to the attorney Cohraine had mentioned. His tactics sounded as repulsive as Joe's scheme.

Johnny gave a deep sigh and turned to go. But another thought stopped him.

He opened his wallet again and found another card with Bill McCollum's name on it. He glanced at the clock. Late Friday afternoon. Bill was an even busier man than Samuel Cohraine, and there was only a small chance Johnny could still catch him at his office.

Still, there was a small chance. Johnny dialed the number and fed coins into the phone.

"Hey, there, Johnny," came Bill's strong voice. "Glad you caught me. I was just wrapping a few things up here before the weekend. As a matter of fact, I was just thinking about you."

Johnny did wonder why Bill might have been thinking about him, but he couldn't spend time dwelling on that question.

Instead, he was dismayed to realize he did not know where to start this conversation. What had he been thinking, in calling Bill? The man on the other end of the line did not know any of the story, nothing of Annie and Joe's history or the current crisis concerning Christine.

"Bill," he began, "I called because I don't know which direction to go and I wanted some wise advice, but now I realize that it would take me an hour to fill you in on the situation, and I'm here on a pay phone, and I guess it might not be a good time to tell you the whole story—" He paused to take a breath.

Bill chuckled.

"I can give you wise advice without even knowing your story, my friend. My advice is to ask someone else. I'm not the one with the wisdom to solve your problem. Ask the heavenly Father. He knows what has to be done, and He's promised us, you know, that He'll give wisdom if we ask for it. It's as simple as that."

"I suppose you're right," Johnny said slowly. "That's what I need to do, Bill. Thank you."

"Sure thing. Hey, I'm headed up your way tomorrow. Hope to stop in and see you and your dad. I'll see you then," said Bill.

Johnny explained that he was not at home, but hoped to be there by tomorrow. Even if he had to stay the night in Indiana, he should be home by early afternoon.

"Oh, well, I do hope to see you," said Bill. "Let me know how that situation, whatever it is, turns out."

20

Mike was doodling in a small notebook when Johnny climbed back into the car. He flipped the notebook shut as Johnny settled back into the seat, but not before Johnny caught a glimpse of a detailed landscape, done in pencil.

"So," Johnny said, using one of Mike's favorite words and at the same time trying to arch one eyebrow just like Mike did, "you're an artist?"

"Not really," Mike replied. "But I like to try to capture some of what I see. It's just something to pass the time.

"So. Where to?" he asked.

Johnny's prayer had been breathed as he walked out to the car. And he felt at peace. He had somehow been started on this road; now he would follow it and see where it led.

"Onward," he said. "That much I know. But which direction do you suppose that might be? Can you read that map?"

Mike gave one short nod.

"I took a look at it. Think I know where we're going." He started the car.

Johnny held the small map and tried to direct Mike as he drove. At least, this area's roads were laid out in straight patterns; the highways didn't twist and bend like they did back home. But as Hank had warned, not every turnoff was marked, and at times they simply guessed as to whether or not they were at the place Hank had marked as a turn.

Johnny watched the farm fields go by, wondering what it would be like to plow, plant, and harvest such large, flat acreage. Did Nappanee have this kind of farms? That young widow his father had talked about—was she left not only with small children, but also a farm like this? But of course, no one would expect Johnny to leave his own farm. In a case like this, the woman's property would most likely be sold or leased, and she and the children would come to Ohio, to the Miller valley.

Johnny shook his head. Why was he even thinking about that? He knew it wasn't going to happen.

They had left the main highway some miles back; the roads seemed to be getting narrower and rougher. One more turn led through a woods. Surprisingly, the road sloped downward as it twisted through the trees. It wasn't much of an incline, but Johnny joked that this was the biggest hill they'd seen for hours. The trees grew close to the road, which had turned to gravel and dirt. It was a beautiful woods, but the road was rough, with large holes.

Mike was driving slowly, trying to avoid the deepest of the holes. The car rattled as it hit one rough spot, and Johnny saw Mike wince, as though the jarring of the car had hurt him.

They came around a sharp bend and Mike hit the brakes hard. It was good he wasn't driving faster, or Johnny would have flown into the windshield.

Within a few feet of them, a truck's bed angled into the roadway. The front of the truck and one tire were wedged deep into the ditch between the trees and the road.

"So. What's this?" Mike said quietly.

At the same time, Johnny caught sight of a body in the roadway beyond the truck.

Mike stopped the car and both men jumped out and hurried around the truck. Johnny reached the prone figure first; Mike limped several paces behind.

The man was lying face down on the gravel, one arm flung out at a strange angle and the other tucked under his body. A tangle of long hair hid his face.

Mike knelt down and gently turned over the body.

Johnny caught his breath. The smell of the man was nauseating. Johnny detected alcohol. He knew that smell well enough. The man hadn't washed for a long while. He had vomited on himself. And there was a strange smell that Johnny couldn't identify.

He was bleeding. At first glance, Johnny could not see an open wound, but there was an alarming amount of blood smeared across the man's face, on his shirt, and in his tangled hair. Mike brushed the hair back from the face, gently, and felt the man's neck, looking for a pulse.

"He's alive. We've got to get him to a hospital." Mike rose and started toward his car.

Johnny looked around at the woods and deserted road.

"How do we get help? Way out here?" he called after Mike.

"We'll have to take him. I remember seeing a sign for a hospital soon after we left the diner."

Mike was in his car, starting the engine. He maneuvered around the back of the truck and pulled the car as close to Johnny and the unconscious man as he could.

"Let's get him in."

Mike tried to get a good grip under the man's arms, and Johnny picked up his feet. It was an awkward load, and they almost dropped the stranger. Getting him into the back seat was even more difficult, but somehow they managed to pull and push him onto the seat. Mike had shoved their bags to one end, and the man lay half on the seat and half on the floor.

"Now," said Mike, looking at the surrounding trees, "we have to get this thing turned around. Help me out here, Johnny."

Along the right-hand side of the road was the ditch that had trapped the truck. The trees grew close on the left-hand side. Johnny stood at the edge of the ditch and called encouragement or caution to Mike as the older man pulled the car forward, backed up, pulled forward an inch or two more, backed up an inch or two more, slowly turning the car in the reverse direction. When it was finally possible to drive back around the truck, Johnny jumped into the car, and Mike started off in the direction they had come.

"You remember how to get out of here?" asked Johnny. It was, he thought, an unnecessary question. If they were lost, they were lost. If Mike did remember, then … well, so. They'd get back to a hospital and find help.

Mike's eyes were on the road. "We'll give it a shot. Nothing else to do."

***

They escaped the woods. That part had been simple. There had been no turnoffs or crossroad to confuse them. They simply drove straight out and did not have to make decisions about which way to turn.

But once they were again driving through the flat farmland, Johnny marveled at Mike's decisiveness. Every now and then, Johnny thought he remembered a house and barn—but the long, straight stretches of road and fields did not give up many memorable landmarks. Mike, though, seemed certain of where he was going and never hesitated or asked Johnny for help.

"You did it!" Johnny exclaimed when, at a crossroad, they spotted a simple sign with the letter "H" and an arrow pointing to their left.

The man on the back seat had not made a sound, but Johnny was very aware of his presence—the rank smell of him filled the car.

They pulled up to the emergency room entrance. Johnny hurried inside, where he found a woman sitting behind a small window. She slid the glass to the side as he approached.

"We need help," he said. "We have a man who was in an accident ..."

She picked up the phone before he had finished, and in seconds, two young men dressed in green scrubs appeared with a gurney and followed Johnny out to the waiting car.

The man in the back seat was still unconscious. In spite of the tension he felt, Johnny had to smile as he watched the two orderlies deftly remove the man from the car and place him on the gurney; he remembered how he and Mike had struggled to get the man into the car in the first place.

The inert body was wheeled off, and Johnny went back to the window. The lady at the desk had very black hair piled high on her head and a pencil stuck into the thick, dark nest.

He could give her no information. They had no idea who the man was. They had found him lying in the road. Johnny gave her his own name and address.

"If necessary, send the bill to me," he told the woman.

Mike had parked the car and came through the door. There was really nothing more they could do, but the receptionist directed them to a small corner with four chairs. They could wait there, if they liked.

Without discussing the decision, both took a seat.

Johnny, though, found it hard to sit and calmly wait. The tension in his body had not been triggered by this unconscious stranger's emergency, but by the hospital scenes around him. The smell of the place, the sounds, the sight of the orderlies—all had taken him back to the night he and Mandy had rushed Annie to the hospital. Then she had been loaded into an ambulance and transferred to another hospital.

Johnny felt cold as he relived the feelings of that night.

Soon a nurse came from the hallway where the gurney had disappeared. She saw Mike and Johnny and greeted them.

"Your friend has no serious injuries. He's got a bloody nose, and he's extremely drunk and high on some kind of drug; we aren't sure yet what he took, but he's going to be out for a while. You can wait if you like, but it may be hours until you can talk to him. We'll keep an eye on him tonight, and if there are no unexpected developments, you can pick him up tomorrow morning."

Johnny hesitated. How could he explain this situation?

"Thank you," he said finally, and then turned to Mike. "We might as well go."

The odor still lingered in the car, and Johnny noticed blood smears across the back seat.

"So?" asked Mike. "Now what?"

"Do we still have time to find Joe's place?" asked Johnny. "Do you think we *can* find our way back?"

Mike cast an eye toward the sun, resting on the roofs of buildings across the street.

"Not sure how long we have before dark, but even if we do find the guy, we probably don't want to arrive and knock on his door after dark. Not the first impression you'd like to make, is my guess."

"So we have to wait until tomorrow." Johnny wondered if this was also a confirmation that he must check on the man at the hospital tomorrow, too. "Well, I guess we can always stay back at that motel next to Mabel's diner. We'll have to find our way there. Besides, we'll want to start there again, anyway, if we're trying to follow this map that Hank drew us." The small paper still lay on the dashboard.

"I have a better idea," said Mike, and he started the engine.

21

"All right," said Johnny. He sat back without another word. He was tired of trying to figure out exactly what he was doing here. He had started this journey to talk with and help the Yoders; then he had sensed a clear directive—was it from God?—to find Joe. But after this twist in the day's plans and the ambush on his emotions by the memories of Annie in the hospital, he wasn't at all certain of the path he was on. Let Mike take the lead for tonight; Johnny was good with that. He was tired.

He closed his eyes and let his mind wander back over all that had happened since Annie's death: his bicycle trip, Samuel and Audrey, the commune and Sydney, Big Bill, his own near-death, the long weeks in the hospital, Maureen, River Man and his miracle of healing, coming home, Audrey and Naomi, Audrey beside him in the road cart, Audrey saying goodbye.

As the people and places of the last few years marched through his mind, he must have dozed, because he jerked awake when the car thumped over a rough spot, and then another and another.

They had turned onto something that felt like a rough field lane. The sun was gone and no moon had replaced it. Out of town, away from streetlights, they were driving through a very dark countryside, with little visible except what appeared in the swath cut through the darkness by the headlights. Johnny could tell, though, that the land was still very flat, but he could see no lights from homes or businesses. He felt completely disoriented.

Where are we?

Mike slowed more, and pulled up beside a looming shape that was even darker than the dark landscape. One small flicker of light was at the center of the darkness.

"So. Guess my memory is better than I thought it was," said Mike with a pleased grin. "Welcome home, for tonight, Johnny."

"Where are we?" asked Johnny.

"Not sure exactly," said Mike. "That is, I don't know what township or address might be attached to this place, but it's a cabin, a small refuge owned by a friend I knew years ago. And since that light is still in the window, it means the place is open for any wanderer who might need shelter for the night. Come on, let's check it out."

The door was unlocked. Mike found a switch right inside the door and flooded the interior with light. It was a cozy cabin with a small kitchenette and table in one corner, a quilt-covered bed against one wall, and a plump couch and chair in front of a stone fireplace. A door stood open to a small room. Johnny glimpsed an old claw-foot tub with a bright yellow shower curtain hung around it. A ladder gave access to a loft.

The room said, *Welcome, Wanderer.*

"You found this place ... in the dark." It was a statement of amazement, not a question.

Mike was still grinning.

"So. When you first told me where you were headed in Indiana, I didn't recognize the town name. But once we got to the hospital, I knew I'd been in this area before. Things started clicking. Like I said, my memory's better than I thought. Nice place, huh?"

"Yes, very nice," replied Johnny. "You're a man of many surprises, Mike."

Johnny caught the glint of light outside a window. On the wall opposite the door they'd come through, another door led outside. He went over, opened it (it, too, was unlocked) and peered out into the darkness.

They were on a very small lake. He could see small points of light on the gently moving water. As his eyes grew accustomed to the darkness, he saw the outline of a fringe of trees around the shoreline.

Mike was hobbling around the kitchen, opening cupboards and the refrigerator.

"So. I was intent on finding this place and didn't even think about supper, but now I'm starved. How about you?"

"Sure," said Johnny.

One cupboard had two shelves filled with canned goods and several plastic boxes holding crackers, cookies, tea bags, and coffee. Before long, the room filled with the aroma of simmering soup.

Paper, kindling, and logs had been carefully laid in the fireplace, ready for a match. Someone had, indeed, prepared a welcome for wanderers. The night was cool, not cold, but Johnny wanted the comfort of a fire. He found matches on the mantle and lit the paper and kindling.

The reds and golds of the fire banished the last of the dark, cold thoughts the hospital had brought on. The soup refreshed him. And Mike's cheerfulness seemed to put the world back in balance.

Johnny found himself returning to curiosity about the man who was helping him.

"How can we thank your friend for his hospitality? Is there some way we can repay him?" he asked, as they finished their soup.

"No, don't think so," said Mike with a grin. "Just enjoy it. And by the way, it's *her*, not *him.*"

"What?"

"The owner of this place is a woman, not a man."

Of course. He should have recognized that from the evidence of the quilt on the bed, the pillows on the couch, the cupboard stocked with food, big towels in the bathroom, even the soup ladle that Mike had found in a drawer full of utensils.

"So what brought *you* here in the first place?" Johnny asked.

"Oh, assignments over the years have taken me here and there. I've covered lots of territory in my time."

Johnny was about to ask what Mike's business was—or had been, since his taxi service for the Amish probably was a sign he was retired—but Mike abruptly stood up and carried dishes to the sink.

"I'll make a deal with you," Mike said, with his back turned to Johnny, "I'll wash up the dishes if you sleep in the loft. I'm not sure my leg will make it up that ladder."

Johnny had forgotten about the loft. He climbed up the ladder to take a look. Sure enough, there was an area large enough to accommodate two more beds, both just as inviting as the one in the main room. As Johnny lay in one of the beds later, he could simply turn his head and have a view of the lake through a high window.

Before he went to bed, he had leaned over the railing of the loft and called a goodnight to Mike. The silver-haired gentleman was sitting in front of the fire, humming to himself, his pencil skimming over a page in the sketchbook.

22

Johnny could hardly believe it when he opened his eyes. The sun was already up; it must be at least seven o'clock. His inner alarm clock had been set to milking time for so long that he was never afraid of oversleeping. But this morning, he had.

It could have been the smell of bacon and coffee that woke him. He took a quick glance over the railing before getting dressed. The room below was empty, but several pieces of bacon lay on a plate on the counter.

Downstairs, he poured himself a cup of coffee and then opened the door to the porch on the lake side of the cabin. Mike sat there in a rustic log chair, his pencil again working on a sketch.

Johnny looked at the scene that seemed to be flowing from the tip of Mike's pencil. A wheat field, ready for harvest. The lines were so skillfully drawn that he could almost see the movement as the wind blew through the field, bending the stalks with their heavy, full heads. Johnny knew that scene; he could *feel* that scene.

He turned and looked out across the small lake, glittering in the morning sun. The few trees around the lake were so sparse that Johnny could see beyond—and the only fields he saw were several just beginning to show green lines of young corn stalks and one large area that looked like pastureland.

"Mike, you told me that you like to draw what you see. I see a lake, not a ripe wheat field."

"Ah, good morning to you, too, Johnny," said Mike without looking up or slowing the movement of the pencil. "We see much more than what is right in front of our noses, you know. And this is what I'm seeing this morning."

He paused then, held the sketchbook up and gave it an appraising gaze, then looked up at Johnny, sipping his coffee.

"So, I saved some bacon for you. There's oatmeal on the stove, too."

"I saw. Thanks."

***

"Mike, you amaze me," said Johnny.

They were pulling into the hospital parking lot. On the drive back to the hospital, Johnny had watched the huge fields and straight highways slip by, and they all looked the same to him. Of course, he had dozed off the night before, and it had been dark, so he had no memory of their route; but Mike had found their way back to the hospital without hesitation.

"Maybe that's why you found me when you did—you needed someone with serious navigational skills." Mike grinned at his passenger.

"Maybe," said Johnny. He peered at the windows of the hospital. "Do you suppose he's called friends or family by now? Maybe he's gone, not even here anymore."

"Only one way to find out," said Mike. He stopped at the emergency room door and waited for Johnny to exit the car, then pulled away to find a parking spot.

Johnny stood for a moment, watching the car. A very strange thing had happened that morning. When he loaded his overnight bag into the back seat, he noticed that all the blood and other stains left by the unsavory stranger were gone. Even the nauseating odor had evaporated. How and when had Mike cleaned that up?

He went inside, stopping at the window. The lady with the black beehive and pencil had been replaced.

"Can I help you?" the new woman asked.

"We're here to check on a man we brought in last night. He was in an accident ... we think."

"Oh, we only had two come in last night, and one ... Umm, let me see ..." she looked through a few papers. "You want the accident victim? Yes, here we are. John Miller. Yes, he's ready to go home."

"I'm John Miller," said Johnny.

The woman looked at him, a faint frown pulling her eyebrows together.

"Hmm. This says the patient is John Miller."

"I gave my name to the lady who was here last night and told her I'd be responsible for the bill, if necessary. But my name is Johnny Miller. I don't go by *John.*"

The creases on her forehead deepened.

"That is strange. We've got the patient's name as John Miller, but I do see a Johnny Miller's name and address here on the bill. Hmm. I wonder how that happened. But of course, you know, being Amish yourself, that here in Amish country there are lots of John Millers. Maybe it's just a really weird coincidence."

She paused, then seemed to dismiss the puzzle from her mind.

"Did you want to pay the bill now?" she asked brightly. "Or we could mail it to you. But I'm afraid you are going to be billed. This John Miller has already informed anyone who will listen that he is *not* going to pay a cent, because he never asked to be brought here. I guess he's given the night nurse an unpleasant night."

"So he must be awake, then," mused Johnny.

"Oh, yes."

"I'll pay now."

The receptionist took his payment and directed him back the hallway. A nurse met him.

"You're here for John Miller?"

Hearing his own name spoken to refer to the dirty, unpleasant stranger gave Johnny a strange sensation, as though he were only a spectator in a play where someone else was taking his role.

"I ... I guess."

"Right this way."

Before she turned to walk down the hall, Johnny stopped her with a question.

"Is his name ... that is ... what did you say his name is?"

"John Miller. At least, that's what he told us. But we suspect he's lying. He didn't say it *convincingly,* you know? There are telltale signs. He doesn't seem to want to be known, and we think the name is just the first one that popped into his head. It's a very common name around here." She looked quizzically at Johnny. "Do you know who he is?"

"No," he shook his head. "No, I don't know him."

"He refused to give us names of any family or friends to call, so I guess you're his only hope."

She led Johnny to a small area with three beds separated by curtains.

Pulling back the first of the curtains, she said, "Mr. Miller, your ride is here."

The man lying on the bed had been washed and his hair brushed back, but his face was the color of Mandy's pie dough, and Johnny noticed the dirty and smoke-stained fingernails. *He looks sick. They should be keeping him here.* It was difficult to estimate the man's age—his countenance had been marked by years that had not been well-lived. He wore the same stained clothes, but it looked like someone had tried to clean those up also.

"I'm not expecting anyone," the man said. His words were almost a growl.

"This man says he's here to take you home," the nurse replied, with a forced cheerfulness.

Well, Johnny thought, *that's not exactly what I said ...*

Then the man caught sight of Johnny, entering behind the nurse. He gave a short, barking laugh.

"This is rich! An Amishman has come to spring me! Unbelievable."

The laugh ended in a fit of coughing.

The nurse looked at Johnny and gave a slight shake of her head.

"You got the buggy outside?" the patient asked.

Johnny looked the man in the eye, calmly, and John Miller looked away.

"No," Johnny said. "I have a driver. We don't know you, sir, but we found you unconscious on the road last night. I stopped in to see if you're all right, and to ask if there's anything more we can do to help you."

The man in the bed looked back at his visitor, then quickly looked away again.

"I've gotta get outta here," he muttered.

"We can take you home, if you like," answered Johnny. "I think we're going your way."

"How would you know where I live?" The tone was instantly cautious.

"I meant, we are going in the same direction you were headed when you had your accident."

John Miller considered this offer and information. He was obviously loath to accept help, especially from the stranger at the foot of his bed, but Johnny guessed that the man did not have any alternative.

23

The man who called himself John Miller was again in the back seat of the car, this time sitting rigid and wary. Johnny had felt strange introducing him to Mike, but Mike simply gave John Miller a nod and Johnny a raised eyebrow.

They were headed back to the starting point on their map, Mabel's diner.

"Anyone hungry?" asked Johnny.

"Sure. It's about that time," answered Mike.

Johnny turned to the man in the back seat.

"Want to get a bite to eat? Did they feed you this morning?"

"Nothing edible."

"Okay, let's stop at Mabel's."

"Don't have my wallet," came the gruff voice from the back seat.

"I'm buying," announced Johnny.

The day before, they had been at Mabel's for a late lunch; now it was just a few minutes before noon, and the parking lot was full. As Johnny opened the door to the restaurant and stepped back to allow Mike and John Miller to enter first, he saw the stranger hesitate, then hunch his shoulders and march in behind Mike with his head down.

The last booth back in the left-hand corner was available. Mike led the way. John Miller took the seat with his back to the full, busy room. His shoulders were pulled up, like someone who huddles against the rain. Johnny and Mike sat down opposite him.

Ellie was there immediately, greeting them and handing them menus.

"The special today is pot roast and apple pie," she said, "unless you want breakfast."

Johnny didn't bother reading the menu. He handed it back to her. "I'll have the special."

Mike did the same, and John Miller shrugged and said, "Okay."

"Great," said Ellie with a smile. She brought three coffee cups and filled them, then disappeared to wait on another table.

The diner was filled with talkative patrons, and the noise rose and enveloped them. It would have been good, Johnny thought, as his eyes roamed across the crowded room, to just sit here and forget about this man's trouble, forget about the hunt for Joe and the confrontation that would come, forget about all that had happened and just enjoy the comfort of this food. But he could not do that. The three sat in a bubble of silence, surrounded by hubbub, and the silence was awkward.

Across the room, Johnny saw a face he recognized. The man who had given him the map to Joe's place was here again, sitting at a table and talking with a man and a lady. Hank had caught sight of Johnny, too, and he gave Johnny a nod.

Someone had to say something. Johnny began.

"Perhaps we can help you get your truck out of the ditch," he said.

"Look, what do you guys want from me?" John Miller sounded hostile. "Why'd you do it?"

"Do what?" asked Johnny. "Take you to the hospital?"

"And feed me. Pay my bill."

"You needed help."

"I don't buy that. I didn't ask for help. But everybody's got an angle. What's yours?"

"Nothing. You needed help. You're hungry."

"We'll get you back to your truck, and maybe we can get it running again," added Mike. "We're here to help."

A hollow laugh came from John Miller's throat. At least, Johnny thought it was intended to be a laugh. *But it sounds like he doesn't know how to laugh any more.*

"That old wreck isn't going anywhere," the stranger said. "Pretty much like my life. There's not much help for me … at least, there wasn't …" He gave a sickly grin, "until a few weeks ago. Things are looking up a little."

Ellie set plates filled with pot roast, carrots, and potatoes in front of them. John Miller was indeed hungry. He attacked the food. Yet he kept his shoulders hunched against the crowd. *Shutting everyone out,* thought Johnny.

"So. Life hasn't turned out quite like you wanted?" asked Mike.

A snort came from across the table.

"You have no idea, mister. Pretty well stinks. Luck's going to change soon, though." He was talking through a mouthful of carrots.

"So? How's that?" asked Mike, lifting a forkful of meat.

"I have a goose that's going to lay a golden egg. That will change things. Life's going to be different."

Mike gave a small smile.

"I thought those birds were all extinct," he said. "Didn't know there were still some around."

"Oh, you just gotta know how to use opportunities," replied John Miller. The food seemed to have opened some door in the surly man. He was suddenly talkative.

"How's life going to be better?" asked Johnny.

"Money. Lots of it." Johnny felt repulsed by the look in John Miller's eyes. Was it greed? Evil?

"Look," the stranger went on, "I'm not some charity case for you do-gooders to pick up. I just need a ride back to my truck. I can handle things from there. Don't go out of your way for me."

"We're headed that way ourselves," said Johnny. "We're looking for a man—"

John Miller jumped when a large, muscular hand came down on his shoulder. He twisted away, to both escape the hand and turn to see who had grabbed him.

"Fritz! It's good to see you, buddy. Where've you been?"

The stranger gave one brief glance up, then looked away. Johnny thought he had the look of a trapped animal.

"Around. What's happened to you? Barely recognized you."

"Met someone," Hank answered cheerfully. "Changed my life. Let's get together sometime, Fritz."

Ellie silently slipped three plates with apple pie onto the table and filled their coffee cups.

Hank nodded at Mike and Johnny.

"Gentlemen. I hope your mission has been successful," he said.

Mike raised one eyebrow at Johnny, indicating that he would leave the response to Johnny.

"Not yet," Johnny said. "But we're still hopeful."

Hank looked thoughtfully at John Miller, who kept his head bent, stirring his coffee.

"Well, it's good to see you, Fritz. Call me. It's been too long."

"You think we'd have much to say?" The words were hostile, spat out. Hank ignored the tone.

"Sure. We have a lot of catching up to do, buddy. Look, let's get together. I'll give you my number." Hank pulled out the small pad in his pocket and scratched out a number.

"Call me," he urged again, handing the paper to John Miller.

The man ignored the offered paper and took a deliberate sip of coffee. Hank laid the paper on the table beside John Miller's plate, nodded to Johnny and Mike, then moved back toward his own table at the other end of the room, stopping several times to greet other diners who seemed to know him.

Johnny was watching the man across from him. His face had deepened to a dull red as he glowered at the piece of pie in front of him. He picked up his fork and began carefully smashing the pie.

Then the stranger swore, tilted his head back, and rolled his eyes.

"How'd he land on his feet?"

An uncomfortable silence followed.

"So. You two are buddies?" Mike asked finally.

"*Were.* Yeah. We go way back. Cousins, actually. We had a few escapades together. You could say we developed all our bad habits together. Got in and out of trouble. Were even in jail together once. Haven't seen him in a few years. I have to say, I'm even surprised to see him here. We took different paths. Looks like he struck it rich along the way, doesn't it? But not everybody's so lucky." The last words were filled with bitterness.

"You referring to yourself?" asked Mike, nonchalantly smearing more apple butter on his bread.

John Miller was silent. His fork smashed a few more apples in the pie. He had not taken one bite of it.

Johnny saw Hank, back at his table, open a Bible as he talked with the couple. He couldn't imagine John Miller ever reading the Scriptures.

"I had a girl once,"—the man's voice was rough—"she was … something happened to her, too. We didn't stay together. But after we split up, she told me she'd fallen in love—with *Jesus!* I don't know what that means, but she had changed."

Johnny could hardly believe what he was seeing and hearing. He had just thought this man to be the most hardened soul he had ever met—but now he heard a soft yielding in John Miller's voice and saw his face relaxing just a bit. The man must have loved that girl.

"I've just never understood that religion stuff. You know how people talk about meeting Jesus and changing their lives? How can that happen? I guess I have to say it really did happen to those two, my cousin and my girl. But it don't seem possible for most of us."

"I don't care how busy they are, it's her job!" a loud, demanding voice snapped. The sharp words came over the back of the booth. "If she can't handle something as simple as coffee, then she shouldn't be here."

The man's voice rose above the hum of the diner noise. A softer, feminine voice attempted more soothing tones.

"And where's the manager? He needs to have more than one waitress at busy times. Tell me why I should pay for this meal if I can't even have coffee," the rant went on.

In one smooth, easy movement, Mike slid out of his seat, took three steps to the coffee pot, and was back at the neighboring booth, pouring coffee and giving the angry man a friendly good morning and how-are-you-doing-today-sir, which was met with a grumbled answer. Then Mike moved on to the next booth and a nearby table, pouring coffee and exchanging greetings with locals who good-naturedly raised their coffee cups to salute him.

Ellie looked up from the table where she was taking an order, met Mike's glance, and gave him a small smile.

But John Miller had opened the door—just a small crack. Shouldn't he, Johnny, take this opportunity to tell him about how God could change worms into beautiful butterflies? That had been the song of Annie's life. But he had never sat in the presence of someone who seemed so bitter and callous, and he felt uncomfortable and uncertain of how to proceed with this conversation.

Mike, I need help here.

Mike was moving to another table with the coffee pot. As though he heard Johnny's thought, he turned to look back at the corner booth and gave Johnny a grin and a thumbs-up.

"John," Johnny began, "the hospital told us your name was John Miller." He felt awkward saying that, using his own name; but still, it was a common name in Ohio, too. There had been another John Miller in his class at school. The church had known several over the years. It was one of the reasons they often identified men by adding their father's name. It could have been only a coincidence.

John Miller was looking at Johnny with a wary look in his eyes.

"But Hank just called you Fritz." Johnny finished.

The stranger seemed to be debating something. Johnny wondered if he might be considering telling the truth.

"Oh, that. That was his nickname for me. He's only a week older than me, but he always called me Fritz as though I was his little brother. We *were* like brothers ..."

For the first time, Johnny noticed the shabbiness of the man's shirt, threadbare around the edges of the collar, a button missing, and stains that had withstood washing.

Mike slid back into the booth.

"So your family's from here?" he asked, picking up the conversation.

The hard voice returned. "Can't say that I have family at all. They've pretty well kicked me out."

"Your cousin seemed glad to see you," said Mike mildly.

John Miller—whoever he was—shoved his pie away with a sudden movement.

"Look, guys, I've gotta get that truck. Can we get moving?"

Johnny was ready to leave, too. The day was slipping away, and he did not want to postpone for yet another day the meeting with Joe.

24

They drove the first few miles in silence. Johnny wanted to concentrate on what he might say when he finally met Annie's old boyfriend—and Christine's father. He had not had much time to think that through, and there was a possibility he would be face-to-face with the man before the end of the day. He felt now as though he should take time to plan how he would approach the subject of his visit.

Instead, his thoughts kept coming back to the conversation at the diner.

It had been only a few days ago that Johnny had read the story of Matthew, a man ostracized by his own people, who Jesus had, even so, invited into His inner circle. "I've come to heal the sick, to help those who know they need help," Jesus had said. Surely this man needed Jesus' healing, just as much as *Johnny* had needed Jesus' healing touch. John Miller and Johnny Miller were much alike in their need for new lives.

And what sad circumstances might have cut John Miller off from his family? Everything in the Amish lifestyle was built on family, church, and community. Even when Johnny had been off on his bicycle ride, not knowing exactly where he was headed or to what kind of life, he knew his family loved and cared about him. What must it be like to know that you cannot go to family for comfort and support because they have turned their backs on you? Except there was Hank, who obviously still wanted to have a friendship with his cousin. Maybe it was John Miller who was shutting everyone else out? What makes a man so bitter, so isolated?

Johnny couldn't remain silent. He half-turned in his seat to look at their passenger.

"You're sure there is no one who is wondering if you're safe? If you're all right? Surely your family would want to know?"

John Miller shook his head and gave one of his scornful snorts.

"Nobody. All I want now is my money. I know of a lawyer who can help me get it. Then I'll get out of here and life will be better."

"Looks like the first thing to do with that money is buy a new truck," commented Mike as they came around the turn and the old truck was still in the roadway, exactly the way they had found it the day before.

"Is it stuck? Or won't it run?" asked Johnny as they all climbed out of the car and approached the dilapidated vehicle adorned with large, rust-eaten holes.

John Miller stared at his truck, at the uncomfortable angle with its nose in the ditch and the rear end jutting into the road.

"I admit I don't remember everything that happened yesterday," he said, "but I do know that when the engine started sputtering and then losing power, I was so mad at the old heap that I floored it and ran it right into the bank. Don't know what I was thinking, maybe that I'd just kill the thing. It's given me enough trouble. Guess now it's both—stuck and dead."

The three stood for a moment, surveying the scene.

"So. Let's see what can be done," said Mike finally. "John, why don't you try to start it. Then we'll figure out how to get it out of there."

The stranger ran his fingers through his long hair, pushing it back from his forehead, then pulled himself up into the tilted cab of the truck. He searched for a moment, then found the keys tossed on the floor. But when he tried to start the truck, there was nothing. He slammed a hand against the steering wheel and started to say something—swearing, Johnny supposed—but caught himself before the words were out.

"Nothing," he said to Mike and Johnny, although it was obvious to them all.

"Let's take a look under the hood," said Mike, "I know a little about engines."

The front bumper of the truck was jammed up against the bank of the ditch, and, although they did get the hood opened, the three had to perch on various precarious spots to peer at the engine. Johnny had driven a car for a few years in his youth, but he had never been interested in learning the mechanics of the machine. He took one look, saw only a complexity covered with years of dirt and grease, and decided he would be of no help.

"I know nothing about this; I have no idea what I'm looking at," he said, jumping away from the awkward stand he had taken straddling the ditch. "What else can I do to help, Mike?"

"Just give me a minute, here …" came Mike's voice. He was fiddling with something.

John Miller stepped away from the truck, too. With a glum look on his face, he stood back and waited.

"Looks pretty firmly wedged in there," observed Johnny.

"Yeah."

A banging came from under the hood. Then Mike's head appeared, "Hey, John, do you have any tools in the truck?"

"No."

"Okay." Mike's head disappeared again.

"You might need a tow truck, to get it out," Johnny said.

"Or I might just leave it right there. There's no hope for that thing. Just like the wreck of my life."

Surprised, Johnny looked at the man beside him.

"There's always hope," Johnny replied.

"No," said John Miller quietly. "I can't see that. You don't know the things I've done. You don't know how I've wrecked my life and the lives of some other people. See, mister, I haven't been one of the good guys—"

Johnny thought he heard a tremor of pain in the gravelly voice.

"The things I've done … people can't forgive or forget." Johnny could hear the hopelessness in his voice. "Not even the money will change some things.

"I was responsible for leading some so-called friends into things that ruined lives. Not just our lives but the lives of people around us. Sometimes, I still see those people in dreams. We partied too much. Drugs. Alcohol. I can't tell you how many lives were affected. It was my fault, I know it. How can any amount of money put back what those families lost?"

Mike was still fiddling under the hood of the truck. Johnny listened to the confessions in stunned silence. *Where was this coming from? Why had this man suddenly decided to pour out his grief and remorse? Now? To him?*

"I told you about my girl … well, there were other girls—a lot. And I used them all. Any girl that I could sweet talk into doing things my way. I was in Canada for a while; things went badly there, too. A girl almost died …"

He kicked at a clump of dirt along the side of the road and then turned and looked down the road, past the truck, in the direction he had once been headed. He went on talking, but never looked back at Johnny. It was as if, Johnny thought, the man wasn't talking to him, but the words had to get out.

"There was one time that I thought maybe I'd get a second chance. Thought maybe I'd get my girlfriend back and we could actually start over and have a real life. We had a child together. I never wanted that baby in the first place, and I had talked Annie into … But she changed her mind at the last minute and wouldn't go along with my plan. She had the baby instead. We broke up. Now, I'm so glad that baby lived—because she's my golden goose. She's going to get me my big payday.

"But it's not going to buy me any peace. I'm not stupid. I know that. That's the last thing Annie ever said to me, that I could find peace with God if I really wanted it, but I laughed her off. I can't forget it, though, and I wish I could ask her about it.

"No, I know the money won't bring me peace or give people back what they lost. But it will at least give me more options than I have now. And my daughter's going to help me get that money."

Johnny felt as though he had been kicked in the stomach. He stared at John Miller's back, and everything else—the truck, the woods, even the road—faded away. He saw only the back of that man in the road and the dirty, tousled hair. He knew he couldn't breathe, and he knew he was going to suffocate.

"So, guys, I don't think we're going to get anywhere with this," Mike said, slamming the hood and coming around the truck. "And there's no way—"

He stopped when he caught sight of Johnny's face. John Miller was standing a few feet away, with his back to Johnny. The man's shoulders were drooping and his head hung forward on his chest. He looked spent; something in him had shriveled up.

Mike looked from one to the other, took a moment, and then said in a low voice.

"You'll have to call a tow truck, John, but we can get you home now."

Neither man moved.

"Come on," Mike said firmly, taking Johnny's arm. "Let's go, guys."

All three moved toward the car, walking mechanically, no one saying a word.

In the car, the man in the back seat said in a subdued voice, "My place is just round the next corner. I was probably trying to walk home when you found me."

Behind the wheel, Mike started the engine, then eased slowly around the truck. In less than a minute, they rounded another sharp curve. To the left, a deeply rutted lane wandered off into the woods.

"Turn here," said John Miller.

Mike glanced at Johnny, then at the small paper with the hand-drawn map, then back at Johnny, with one eyebrow raised.

Johnny nodded, looking straight ahead, his jaw tight.

25

Johnny felt the roughness of the roadway, *felt* rather than *saw*. He saw nothing of the woods they passed through as they crept up the narrow lane, with Mike trying to stay out of the deep ruts and occasionally maneuvering around a branch lying where it had fallen. An old fence ran along the lane, weathered gray and missing a plank here and there. Johnny even missed the fox that was crossing the lane with a small rodent in its mouth and, surprised by the car, darted into the underbrush.

This is Joe. This is the Joe that Annie partied with and fell in love with. How could she have ...? His mind could not put the picture together. He could not imagine the lovely, kind, gentle woman he had married—with this man!

This is the man Annie had a child with. He's Christine's father. Christine's father! What would happen to a little girl, already heartbroken by the loss of mommy and daddy, if she were taken away by this man?

This is the man who treated Annie so horribly and now wants to use a little child for his own schemes. This is the man. And he's sitting in the back seat and we have helped him and fed him and ... now what do we do with him?

Lord, why did you make it THIS man?

He felt sick, as though a poison had been injected into his body and it was working its way through his arteries and veins. Annie had told him about this man. One time she had even left him, Johnny, to go back to Joe—or at least, to talk to Joe about the possibility of their renewing their relationship.

When she left me that night, this is the man she was going to see. She loved me, but she went to see Joe because he was Christine's father. This is the man who wanted to marry her and make a life for her. What kind of life would Annie have had if she had married him?

But of course, it had not turned out that way. Annie had already decided to turn and follow Jesus by that time. She was a changed woman, a worm that God had transformed into a beautiful butterfly, she liked to say. By that time, she could no longer live in the ways she used to live.

She couldn't live with a man like this. She couldn't live with John Miller because ...

The whirling thoughts and emotions were stopped, suddenly, by one clear declaration.

John Miller is not so different than Johnny Miller. If it were not for God changing me, I could have been the one lying dead drunk in the road.

He remembered the pile of beer bottles in the field along the fence row, just down from his tree house. He remembered the morning of the awful crash that crushed a young life. He remembered the hopelessness that he had felt, until he cried out his anguish and asked God to help him.

Johnny had once felt the hopelessness, too—a hopelessness just like Joe's.

***

Before any building entered their view, three large, baying hounds came tearing down the lane to meet them. They yapped and yelped and danced around the car, as though they were an official escort. Mike drove slowly, his head swiveling from side to side, trying to see where all three dogs were.

"They'll stay out of the way. You don't need to worry," said John Miller.

The house seemed to be huddling at the edge of an opening in the woods, yet it was a large, two-story farmhouse with a long porch running the length of the second floor. The elements had worn away all color the house once knew, and wind and rain had slowly pried loose both shutters and shingles. The area in front of the house had been a spacious lawn; now it was overgrown by a tangle of grasses and briars. Barely visible above the brush was a stone wall that must have once been the foundation of a barn.

Mike stopped the car at the foot of the stairs going to the front porch. One of the steps had broken loose on one side, and dangled from a nail that still held it.

The hounds were jumping up on the sides of the car, still barking. Inside the car, no one said a word.

Then John Miller—Joe—gave a deep sigh and said, "Home sweet home."

He opened the back door.

Now what? I came here to see this man, but now what, Lord? I need help! I don't know what to do. I don't know if I even want to be here. I might regret thinking I wanted to meet this man.

Mike had nothing to say. He waited.

Johnny craned his neck to look back at Joe, still standing at the open door.

"What else can we help you with? Can we get someone to pull that truck out of the ditch? Is there someone we can find to come help you?" he asked. He was surprised to hear that his voice sounded ... *natural.*

Joe was shuffling his feet, pushing a rock around with the toe of his boot. The three dogs, content that their master was home, suddenly lost interest in the car and loped off, around the back of the house, into the woods.

"You guys want a beer or something?"

"Coffee would do," said Mike. "I assume it's safe to get out?"

What might have been a smile broke Joe's face.

"Sure. They won't bother you."

The three men carefully climbed the aging stairs to the porch. Joe led the way, and Mike followed. Johnny eyed the treads, wondering if the sagging stairway would hold the weight of all three of them at the same time. He waited until Joe was on the porch floor, then started up himself, carefully taking a long step over the one missing board.

"Hey, Jo—" he caught himself. Already, his mind and tongue were confused.

Do I tell him I know his name is not John? How do I tell him that? Then I'd have to explain how I know and who I am and why I'm here. Or does he already know? No, he couldn't. How would he know? Does he even know who Annie married?

"I could nail this thing down for you, if you want," he called up the stairs.

John Miller hesitated, then shrugged.

"Sure, go ahead if you want."

"Got a hammer?"

"There are some tools on a workbench downstairs."

Johnny went back down the stairs and around the front of the house to a doorway under the porch. The door creaked open.

The interior was shadowy. He could see a single bulb hanging from the ceiling, with a long chain attached. He pulled the chain, and the details of the room came into view.

It had at one time been a summer kitchen. An old stove standing against the wall, a Formica-topped table covered with boxes and piles of papers, and three chairs also holding piles of papers gave evidence of another life at another time. At the far end of the long room, someone had set a rough workbench. There, Johnny found a hammer. Several boxes held nails and screws of various sizes. They were all old; some were even rusted or bent. He picked out a handful of the best. Surely they were better than whatever might still be hanging in the boards of the stairs.

He carried the hammer and nails outside, glad for something to do so that he could postpone going up the stairs and talking with or even being in sight of Joe. How could Annie have loved this man? He wanted to ask her to explain, but he knew he could not.

He knelt on the stairs and pounded in nails with far more force than was necessary. The blows shook the entire stairway. He struck the board again and again and again.

The hammer meeting steel and wood sent a vibration through his body that at first felt satisfying. Then, unexpectedly, he thought of the nails that pinned Jesus' hands to a rough board. He shuddered at the thought of being the one to wield the hammer and having to do such a deed. And then he was given a small glimpse of what it would be like to die in the same way Jesus died. The comprehension, limited though it was, jolted him. He paused, resting the hammer on the stairway.

He was truly human, like me, and he died a terrible, painful death. For me. Even though I didn't deserve it. And He did that for Joe, too.

He remembered the cross that Bill McCollum had erected at the site where he, Bill, had met Jesus.

The cross makes all the difference. That day at the cross ... the blood flowed down ... Jesus' love changed me ... and that makes all the difference, he thought.

"Hey, beer and coffee's all I got. Unless you want water."

Joe's voice came from above his head, and Johnny, pulled out of his reverie, realized he smelled coffee brewing. This was unexpected.

"Sure. Coffee," he called back.

Joe found chairs inside and brought them out to the porch. They sat with their coffee, looking out over the tangled underbrush. The dogs had vanished as abruptly as they had appeared.

"Coffee's good," said Mike with satisfied appreciation.

Joe grinned.

"That's one thing I can make. That, and I can fry myself an egg and bacon."

They sipped in silence, each combing through their own thoughts. Johnny wondered if Annie knew what was happening. Could she see them now, sitting here on Joe's dilapidated porch, wondering what to say to each other? What would Annie say to him now? What would she say to *Joe* if she could talk with him again? Johnny listened for her voice.

There was nothing.

Annie was the one thing that had brought him here, because Annie had told him Christine would need his help. Annie was the connection the two men shared. If Annie had made a different choice—if she had chosen Joe instead of Johnny—then how might their lives be different?

No, the key had not been a choice between Joe or Johnny. The key had been the choice of *Jesus.* To follow Him through life. With that choice made, God had changed Annie. And then He also changed Johnny. Could he even change a man like Joe?

Audrey's voice came then.

"What God is really interested in is changing people's hearts so that they're ready to live in His new world."

Something—Someone—asked a question.

Do you believe I can?

Johnny glanced over at the man they had found passed out in the road. The one who had sworn at them and lied to them and confessed to tearing apart people's lives. The man he had found so repulsive.

He answered the question.

I believe it, Lord Jesus. I do believe it.

But, he added, humbled, *You'll have to make another change to my heart, too.*

26

He could not, though, believe the picture he surveyed in less than an hour. Joe was standing at the stove (grease-splattered and dirty), cooking bacon and frying eggs. They'd been invited to supper.

Johnny never would have imagined this scene.

They had been ushered into the house. Everything inside was old and dusty. On certain pieces of furniture—like a desk in the corner of the kitchen—Johnny could see that Joe had simply used his hand to swipe away some of the dust. The house smelled closed-up and musty.

Wouldn't Mom love to get at this place, Johnny thought with an inward smile, remembering how enthusiastically Mandy tackled the job of transforming *dirty* into *neat and clean.*

When Joe's back was turned, Johnny picked up the fork on the table beside his plate and gave the tines a vigorous wiping with the fabric of his shirt.

Joe had not been exaggerating. He did make a good plate of bacon and eggs. Together, the three of them downed eight eggs and a pound of bacon.

"Good supper, John," said Mike, picking up his plate and fork and carrying them to the sink. The sink and countertop were filled with dishes that, Johnny guessed, had been waiting at least a week to be washed.

That look came over Joe's face—the look that Johnny had come to think of as wary and undecided. As though Joe were trying to make up his mind, but he was afraid to make a choice.

"Look …" Joe started. He hesitated, then plunged ahead. "Look, guys, I have to level with you about something."

His guests waited for him to go on.

"Look, my name's not John. And not Miller. I just used those because the hospital insisted on my giving a name. My name's Joe."

Johnny gave a nod of acknowledgment. Mike offered an offhand "Oh," as though it made no difference to him whether the man was Joe or Pete or Steve.

"Well, just wanted to clear that up," said Joe hurriedly, gathering his own plate and fork and coffee cup. He seemed embarrassed. "Oh, but the story about Fritz being a nickname—that was the truth."

Dusk was falling. Somewhere, way back in the trees, the dogs had found a scent. Their baying echoed through the quiet of the woods.

"Well, should we get going?" asked Mike, raising one of those silver eyebrows at Johnny. "So we can find our way out of here before it gets too dark?"

No, wait. I haven't had a chance yet to tell him … I don't know what I want to tell him, but I know our conversation is not done. We can't go yet.

"Where are you headed tonight?" asked Joe. "Hey, remember back at the diner, you started to tell me that you were looking for a man in this area—but you never did tell me who. I don't know many people around here, kinda keep to myself, but maybe I can help you."

"I think I've given up that mission … Joe." Johnny found the name difficult to voice. "Maybe we were just here to help you, sent down this road at the right time."

Joe shifted his weight and turned away, moving dishes around in the sink.

"Maybe. I guess I should thank you for everything."

"I'm not only good with a hammer, I'm good at dishes, too," said Johnny. "I'll do dishes, if that's okay." The reluctant half of his mind said, *What are you saying? Do you see that pile?*

More hesitation from Joe. Then he agreed.

Joe pushed all the scraps from the dishes—some almost unrecognizable—onto one plate and set it outside for the dogs. Johnny ran the water until it was as hot as his hands could bear, looked for dish soap but found only hand soap, and plunged into the job.

"My wife used to say that it's therapeutic to get your hands into hot dishwater—even for men," he said, attempting a joking tone.

"You have a wife?" asked Joe. "Oh, of course. You've got a beard."

"*Had* a wife. She died," Johnny said quietly.

He could feel Joe's eyes on him.

"I'm sorry," the man replied.

"It was an accident in the barn."

Joe said nothing, and Johnny concentrated on scrubbing off egg that had been on a plate for days.

Mike spoke up.

"Joe, what are you going to do about transportation? You live way back in here, how are you even going to get help with your truck?"

"I won't get any help tonight, that's for sure," began Joe. "Nobody in town will be working on a Saturday night. But first thing Monday, I'll walk down the road a bit. There are Amish neighbors not too far away, and they have a phone booth at the end of their lane. I use it when I need to make calls. I'll call the guy in town that normally works on that junk heap." His voice turned morose. "He'll probably tell me just to junk it. Last time I took it in, he said it was the last time he wanted to see it. Said it was a lost cause, and the only thing I could do was get a new engine."

"Hmm," Mike pondered this, but offered no solution. "Well, at least you've got a phone nearby. I thought maybe we were leaving you stranded far from civilization. Hey, Johnny, I'd offer to help, but looks like you've got everything under control."

"I have," said Johnny.

Mike and Joe moved back to the long porch, and as they exited, the three dogs bounded up the stairs and Joe opened the door to let them into the kitchen. They scrambled under and around the table, licking up every small crumb they could find.

Johnny was so absorbed in thought, he did not notice the dogs. He was thinking about the truck Big Bill had been driving the day they had met at the cross in Texas. It was a dilapidated, beat-up old thing that Johnny had taken as a sign that Bill was a destitute soul. As it turned out, Bill had raised the hood on that antique truck to show Johnny a shiny new engine.

"I'm going to take a short walk while you're finishing up in there," called Mike. "I don't need to feel guilty about going off and leaving the work to you, do I?"

"Nope," Johnny called back.

He was thinking about new engines.

***

Mike was nowhere to be seen when Johnny joined Joe on the porch a few minutes later.

"Can he get lost in these woods?" he asked Joe.

"Nah, no matter which way he goes, he'll walk out of them soon," Joe answered.

Johnny remembered then that Mike had mentioned his superior navigational skills. He decided to trust that Mike would not wander too far and could find his way back. Still, the evening was darkening, and the woods surrounding the tired house and tangled field seemed to hasten the fall of night.

"I still don't get why you guys did what you did for me," Joe said, and Johnny heard a different tone in the man's voice.

"You needed help. We were there," Johnny replied.

It was dark enough that he could not see Joe's face clearly, but he could not miss the sadness in the voice that came out of the dusky evening.

"I think I'm beyond help."

"No one's beyond help."

Now the voice was angry.

"Have you not been listening to me? Haven't you heard what I've said? I've done terrible things. I've been a terrible person. My life's a wreck. Even that money isn't going to change those facts."

About that money—

That's what Johnny wanted to say. Those were the words that jumped to his mind.

But he heard other words come out of his mouth:

"God can give you a new life. I believe that. It happened for me. It happened for my wife, before I met her. It can happen for you, if you want it."

"I don't think God would have any use for me," said Joe, sounding beaten. "I'm sure he'd rather squash me than do anything for me. And I'd deserve it."

"We all deserve it. None of us are good enough to earn God's love or blessings. But He loves us anyway. Like … like a father and mother love a rebellious child."

"I know the words," said Joe. "I grew up in the Amish church. Did you guess that? Well, I did. And I heard the words, over and over again. But I couldn't quite believe them. Why should God forgive me for the things I've done?"

"He'll forgive you because the penalty has already been paid for what you've done. Jesus took your punishment, Joe. Whatever you've done—he took the punishment for it, all of it. Jesus did that so you can come to God and ask for a new life without carrying the guilt."

"A new life ... that would be ... nice." Johnny heard a catch in the voice coming from the other chair.

"God promises He'll do it."

There was a pause. Then Johnny went on.

"You know, I heard you and Mike talking about the engine in your truck. I met a man once who was driving a truck that looked just as bad as yours. But he gave me a look under the hood, and he had a completely new engine. He's been driving that truck for over 20 years. That new engine makes all the difference. That's what God does for people who come to Him for help—it's like He puts a new engine in you—a new heart. And a new heart is the start of a new life."

Joe was quiet for a long while. Johnny did not know what else to say to the man, so he sat in silence, too.

The hounds were hunting again. Their mournful wails came from far off in the woods.

Finally Joe moved in his chair. It creaked.

"It would have to be a miracle," he said in a low voice.

"Yes," Johnny replied. "But God keeps His promises, whether it takes a miracle or not. And, you know, being God, He's quite capable of the miracle stuff."

Joe gave one of his snorts, but it wasn't as derisive as usual.

"Yeah, I guess so. It's just ... kinda unbelievable."

"Yes, it is," Johnny replied softly. "It's unbelievable that He would do that for me. I have to tell you that there was a time I wondered if there was any hope for me ... or if I was a lost cause and nothing about my life would ever be right. But then I found that with God, we can have great hope."

"You can say that," retorted Joe. "You aren't in my shoes."

"No, but my life was … well, I needed a new life, too, just as much as you do. I was supposed to be growing up and becoming responsible; instead, everything in my life was on a downhill skid."

"But you turned into an Amishman and saved yourself."

"Nope. I did end up choosing that lifestyle. But that's not what saved me. That's not what gave me a new engine and changed my life."

"What did pull you out of it?" Johnny knew from the voice that Joe was listening intently.

"I decided to do things God's way. I'd been so stubborn and determined to do things *my way*—but I made a terrible mess of it. So I decided to let Jesus lead me through life. Decided to do it, not because I felt guilty or I was afraid of punishment, but because I wanted so much to have a new life and be a new man. And I knew I couldn't do it myself. Only a miracle could give me that."

"And He did it." Joe ended the story.

"Yes," Johnny found himself smiling into the darkness. "Yes, He most certainly did."

27

If the scene at the supper table had been almost unbelievable, the scene later that night, as Johnny cautiously tried the mattress on a bed in the old house, seemed even more astonishing. Here he was, spending the night at Joe's house! How had this happened?

Oh, Annie, what would you say if you knew? Or do you know? He wondered if she would be laughing happily and saying, *Miracles, dear. That's what God does.*

As Johnny had felt his conversation on the porch with Joe coming to an end, he rose, wondering where Mike might be. Full darkness had fallen. Above the clearing, the Milky Way and thousands of other stars were brilliant. But how would Mike find his way back?

Johnny went to the railing of the porch and strained to see through the darkness. It was useless. He could see nothing except the dark ring created by the trees around them.

Going to the stairway, he was startled to see a figure sitting on the first step below. The dogs lay quietly at Mike's feet, and he was stroking the head of one of them. Just sitting there, waiting for the conversation above to draw to a close.

Then the impossible had happened. Joe, awkwardly, had invited them to stay, telling them there were five bedrooms upstairs, none in use. Joe slept in the one bedroom downstairs. They could take their pick of any of the upstairs rooms.

And they had accepted.

Johnny sat down on the bed and pulled off his shoes. He thought maybe he'd just sleep in his clothes that night … and maybe on top of the bedspread.

***

He woke much later, slightly chilled. Moonlight was falling through the window, and outside, the night looked bright.

He heard pacing downstairs. A chair scraped along the floor. One of the dogs was pacing, too. The house was so quiet that he could hear the sound of the dog's nails clicking on the linoleum. Water running. More walking. Joe must have been up.

Johnny could not stay awake long enough to wonder. He could not stay awake. He pulled the quilt around his shoulders and over his body and went back to sleep.

***

The next morning, bacon was again frying and the percolating coffee smelled wonderful. Johnny went downstairs to find Mike already at the breakfast table and Joe once more at the stove.

Good mornings were said all around, but when Joe turned around, Johnny was taken aback.

The man's face was haggard—he obviously had not slept the night before, or, if he had, it had been very little. Yet he was changed—he had combed his long hair and pulled it back into a ponytail. He had shaved, and maybe even showered. His shirt looked brand new; in fact, it still bore the creases from being neatly folded, just as it had come from a store.

Mike raised an eyebrow at Johnny.

"Joe's just telling me that he wants to be going somewhere this morning. I thought maybe we could accommodate him, since we're going back into town anyway."

Johnny looked at Joe quizzically.

"I need to go to church," Joe said firmly.

***

The drive back to town seemed shorter than before. John Miller, who had been in the back seat, now seemed forgotten. It was Joe in the back seat. This morning he was shifting constantly, as though he could not find a comfortable spot, smoothing his shirt, and every now and then pulling his ponytail tighter. Then he moved his hands, seeming to look for someplace to rest them but finding none. His boots wiggled, and Johnny heard a sigh from the back seat at least once every mile.

They let Joe direct them. He knew of a church, he told them. It had been there forever. There were five or six congregations in town, but he would go to this one. It was on the edge of town, it was small, and, as far as he knew, no one there would know him— all good factors, Joe had decided.

It was indeed a small church. The parking lot was on one side, and the church cemetery on the other. It looked like most of the congregation had moved to the cemetery. Less than a dozen cars were lined up in the parking lot. The sign outside said the worship service started at 11:00. They drove in at 10:45.

Mike stopped the car. No one moved.

Johnny wasn't sure what was happening. Were they going to the service, too? He and Mike had not discussed the possibility. They had simply cleaned up that morning, eaten breakfast, and gotten into the car to drive Joe—to church!

He heard Joe take a deep breath.

"Well, might as well get in there," Joe said with a sudden movement, opening the door and almost jumping out of the car.

Johnny opened his own door and stepped out. Joe looked at him, and then he stretched out his hand.

Johnny shook the offered hand, marveling at what was happening.

"Thank you," said Joe. "For everything. I don't know what brought you here to begin with, but I'm glad I was lying in the road in front of you. Now this—" he waved toward the church. "This is something I've got to do myself."

"Okay," said Johnny, looking Joe in the eye. "Remember, God delivers new engines."

A small smile broke the deep lines on Joe's face.

"I'll remember. I'm counting on it."

He started toward the church, then stopped and turned back to Johnny.

"I don't even know your name."

"Johnny. Just Johnny. That's enough."

Joe nodded and raised his hand in one more farewell. He looked toward the gold cross on the simple, white door.

Three steps led up to the landing in front of the door, and as Joe reached the bottom of the steps, he hesitated. He was going to turn around and come back to the car. Johnny felt a wave of disappointment and sadness.

But in that moment, the door opened and a man stepped out onto the landing. He was startled to see Joe standing there, but his surprise was swept away by joy when he recognized his cousin. Whatever mission had prompted him to step outside was forgotten in his excitement.

"Fritz!"

Hank bounded down the stairs and grabbed Joe in a bear hug. He kept his arm around his cousin's shoulders, talking excitedly as they started up the steps. Joe glanced back at Johnny, an incredulous look on his face.

Johnny was just as astonished as Joe. A huge smile broke through his beard as he got back into the car and turned to Mike.

"Let's go home."

28

"But what about Christine?" Mandy leaned forward, ignoring her breakfast.

Johnny was reporting to his parents all that had happened over the three days he had been gone. He had awakened in his own bed that morning, long before the normal time to milk. While it was still dark, he had dressed and gone to the barnyard.

The cows were already waiting at the gate. He called a soft hello to his horse, Joyce, grazing in the pasture, and she nickered a greeting. As he opened the door of the chicken house, a few early birds ran down the walkway. The rooster wasn't among them. Johnny grinned; he had had to wake the rooster. Upstairs in the barn, a sweet aroma told him that new hay had been brought into the hay mow. Maybe Paul had been over to help his father.

It was good to be back.

John, surprised to find his son in the barn before him, greeted Johnny heartily. John's wise eyes searched Johnny's face without voicing his question. Johnny smiled at his father.

"I'll tell you and Mom all about it at breakfast."

And so he had. But he could not tell them the ending of Christine's story. No one except her Heavenly Father knew what that ending might be.

"What will happen, do you suppose?" asked Mandy.

"I don't know. But I couldn't talk to Joe about it, as I had thought I would. God obviously has plans for that man—plans other than *my* arguing him out of whatever he wants to do. But I was—I *am*—convinced that God has started working in his life, and so I am going to trust that God is also going to take care of Christine."

Mandy sat back in her chair, and Johnny thought that the look on her face was perfectly peaceful. But there were tears in her eyes, too.

"You know," he went on, "I always thought Annie's words meant that it was Christine who would need me. But maybe God's intention was that I help Joe, instead. Maybe that's the real reason I had to go to Indiana."

He could imagine how Annie's eyes would have sparkled at this and how delighted she would have been as she repeated one of her favorite sayings: *God works in mysterious ways, dear.*

The thought of Annie brought a small wave of discomfort. He had to admit it—the last few days had raised some questions about his wife's past.

"There's something I'm wondering about …" he began. Then he was not sure he wanted to go on. Mandy leaned forward again, listening for his next words.

He decided to plunge into the thoughts that had been nagging at his heart. "When I talked to Samuel Cohraine, he started to say something about Christine's birth certificate, and then we were interrupted. But I'm sure he was trying to say that Joe's name wasn't on the birth certificate. How could that have happened? I can't figure that out."

Mandy sat up straighter, then rose and carried her plate and silverware to the sink. Her son and her husband weren't fooled.

"Mandy, do you know something about that?" asked John.

She turned to them, wiping her hands on a towel and rolling her eyes, attempting to make light of whatever it was she knew.

"Only that Annie gave the hospital a fictitious name. She confessed that to me once. She was sorry she had done it, but it was a tactic to get back at Joe, I think," Mandy said.

"A fictitious name?" asked Johnny, frowning.

"Yes. No one she knew. She just didn't want to give Joe any credit in the matter, because he had ... behaved so badly toward her and ... the baby." She picked up Johnny's and John's plates and went back to the sink, busying herself with rinsing the dishes.

"That would explain why Samuel said Joe probably doesn't have a chance if the case goes to court. He would have no proof he was Christine's father," said Johnny. "And he probably doesn't even know about the birth certificate."

"I'm sure they can find witnesses that knew Joe was dating Annie and that Annie had named him as father, regardless of what was on the birth certificate," said John. "But, true, then they will simply have to build a case on what people thought and said."

"Let's hope it never gets to that," said Mandy over her shoulder. Her hands were in the dishwater, and her back was to the men at the table.

There was something else.

It sat, like some shadowy, shapeless monster, in a corner of Johnny's memory. For the last two days, he had been refusing to look at it, as if looking at the dark threat might give it more power. Maybe, if he ignored it, it would slink away.

But it had not left his consciousness. As a matter of fact, it was growing in size. He did not want to acknowledge it now, but he felt compelled to do so, here, in the company of two people he trusted so much.

"One more thing—" He stopped and cleared his throat, unsure of what to say next.

"Joe mentioned ... that is, he said ... he told me he never wanted the baby, and that he had other plans, and he implied that if they had carried out his plan, Christine would not be alive today.

He said … apparently, Annie was going along with what he wanted. Until the last minute. Then she backed out."

He finished, miserable. Saying the terrible words aloud, here, in the sanctuary of this home that had always cherished and nurtured love and family, made it feel as though evil had breached the walls of home, and it made his words all the uglier.

Mandy choked back a sob. She turned from the sink to face Johnny, and now her eyes were not only full, but overflowing.

"But she didn't do it. She thought about the life within her, she had even named the baby, and she couldn't do it," Mandy said.

"Mom …" Johnny stared at her. "Mom—*did you know?*"

Mandy nodded. Her voice was full of love for the daughter-in-law she had lost. "She told me, before you were married."

Stunned, Johnny stared at his mother, but he was seeing the face of his beloved Annie, trying to put this information into the story of his wife's past. It had been hard enough to imagine her with Joe, but this—

"She never told me."

"I'm sure she was going to," said Mandy gently. "Maybe she just never found the right time or the right way to tell you."

"Maybe she wasn't going to tell me at all." He felt somehow betrayed. "Maybe she wanted to leave all that behind her and close the book on it. You know, she was always quoting that verse about God transforming us into new creatures and *The old is gone.* Maybe she did not want to ever think about it again, and she never intended to tell me."

"Don't forget the rest of that Scripture, son," interjected John. "*The new has come.* That's what you and Annie shared. The new lives God gave you both. That's what you lived together. Not the old. The old truly *is* gone. It was for Annie. We know that. Let it be gone for you, too."

29

Following the horses in the hay field the next day, Johnny would ponder that conversation and the conversations with Joe. He would come to a place of new understanding of his beautiful bride and her adamant, unwavering declaration of God's power to change lives. As this new picture of Annie came into focus, he began to have a better understanding of the burden of guilt she had carried and then gave to God when she asked His forgiveness at the cross of Jesus. He saw more fully the reason Annie had glowed when she spoke of the One who rescued her, the Jesus she loved.

He thought of her almost constantly as he mowed the south hay field and the sun burned the back of his neck and his forearms. He would never know the reason she had not told him about the plan for aborting her baby, but he did not need to know. By the time the field was mowed, he looked across the waves of cut hay and had little memory of the physical labor he had done there. But at the end of the day, he could also say that the old was gone. The new had come. And that was enough.

As he was unhitching the big Belgians, a car drove up the driveway, stopped, and John emerged. Seeing Johnny, he set his briefcase beside the hitching post and came to the barn to help.

"You're back early," said Johnny.

"The bank had all the paperwork ready. I didn't have to wait, and there wasn't much to be done except sign at all the right places," said John.

"Something's on your mind, though," observed Johnny, as he looked at his father across the broad back of one of the Belgians.

"Last night, Mom and I were so caught up with your story about your trip that we forgot to tell you our news," replied John. "Bill McCollum stopped in unexpectedly on Saturday."

"Bill! I'm sorry I missed him. When I talked with him on the phone, he did tell me he was coming up. Was he back in town to see about that real estate?"

"Yes, it looks like the deal is going through. I must say, once he decided that he wanted that acreage, it didn't take him long to make things happen."

Johnny chuckled. Yes, that was Big Bill.

"He stopped in to see me—and he was hoping you'd be here, too—to talk about hiring and working with Amish people. He's hoping many of our community will work for him, and he wanted to know how to make that happen. He's not going to run the plant on Sunday, and he's promised that Amish employees will be able to take the day off to observe our religious days. I have to respect that man—he cares about his work force. While I hate to see a beautiful 40 acres go to building a factory, I also have to say that I think it will be a good thing for our county."

Johnny was brushing the Belgian's muscular neck. He waited. He knew there was more on his father's mind than the county's economy.

"He wanted to talk with you and me about jobs."

"What?" Johnny's gaze jerked to his father's face.

"He's looking for a plant manager. Someone who would be involved in this project from the very start. First, as project manager for the building phase; then to actually manage the plant.

That person would be Bill's representative here as the construction goes along."

"Would you be interested in that?" asked Johnny, watching his father's reaction. He noticed that John's hair was still dark, but his beard was rapidly graying. His father could not keep up the physical labor required by the farm and the logging business forever—maybe this would be a good change for him.

"You're not?" asked John.

Johnny almost laughed. Work in a factory? No. No, that was one of the last things he'd consider doing. He loved the soil and growing things. He wanted to experience the seasons in the outdoors, not looking through an office window. Besides, his dad was a far better businessman than Johnny would ever be.

Yes, he still felt that restlessness. As much as he loved his farm, he sometimes looked across his fields and felt that there was *something* more, something waiting for him. He just had not yet discovered what that was. But one thing he did know—it wasn't a factory job, no matter how high up in management the position might be.

"No," he answered. "Not for me."

He could feel his father's eyes on him. So there was still something more. He waited.

"Bill has another job for you. He wants to offer you a job with his mission network."

"What?"

"They've got so many projects that they're supporting right now—and also starting new ones—that he is creating a new position. He needs someone to work with agricultural programs in areas where they feel they can make a difference."

"In *areas* ... you mean, around the world?" Johnny was incredulous. Bill McCollum had a pact with the Lord. He had promised to give 90 percent of his company's profits to missions, and he had been doing just that for many years. McCollum's 90 Percent Project supported mission work in many countries.

"Yes," said John, quietly.

"That's impossible. I've got a farm to tend. You've always said we are stewards of the earth. And my stewardship is right here. Besides, I'm not going around the world in a buggy or by bus. I'd have to fly. And we don't fly," said Johnny.

"He's aware of all that."

"What did you tell him?" Johnny asked.

"You mean, about the factory job or about the offer he's going to make you?"

"Both, I guess."

"I told him I'd think about the plant manager's job. If God wills that I move into a new season in life, it might be a good thing. And I told him he'd have to talk with you about the ... other offer."

"I don't understand why he'd ask that of me," said Johnny. "He knows, doesn't he?"

"He knows," replied his father.

John gave a parting stroke to the white-blazed forehead of the Belgian and then walked toward his briefcase and the house.

30

The week went by, and Johnny soon slipped back into the familiar routines. He cut and raked hay, finally planted the last of the corn, and every now and then caught a glimpse of his nephew Simon slipping up to the tree house.

Johnny's three older sisters and Naomi came over one day to help Mandy quilt, and Johnny heard them talking about a letter Naomi had received from Audrey. They talked, too, about the rumor going around the community that a factory was coming to the county, and how folks were already speculating on how it might affect their lives.

Johnny thought often of Joe and prayed for God's continued transformation of Joe's heart and life. He was still amazed at the entire sequence of events that had led them to that small church on Sunday morning.

He was also amazed at the transformation of his own thoughts about the man who had shared such a sordid part of Annie's past. Now he had a growing, genuine concern for Joe's heart and eternal soul. He hoped that Hank had taken Joe under his wing. Wouldn't Annie be surprised to see Joe marching through the gates of Heaven? She would be delighted. *Or maybe,* he thought, as he tried to imagine what heavenly life was like, *maybe she already knows.*

At the supper table on Friday night, Mandy had several pieces of mail. One was a newsletter from Audrey's orphanage—or, the orphanage where Audrey worked. They had begun to refer to it as "Audrey's orphanage."

Audrey had written a short note to the family, thanking them for their hospitality the week before Naomi's wedding and telling them she was back in Mexico, delighted to be with "her" children again. That was all. Nothing more personal than a thank-you to the entire family. Johnny had to admit that he was a little disappointed. But, he reasoned, that was for the best.

The second was a letter from Indiana, from the Yoders, Annie's parents.

"What do they have to say?" asked John, as he sat down to supper.

"I didn't open it. I thought I'd wait until you were both here. I certainly hope it's good news," said Mandy.

They waited until the meal was finished to open the letter. John picked it up, sliced it open with his knife, and began reading aloud. Then he stopped and quickly scanned the rest of the letter, continued on the back of the page, without reading to Johnny and Mandy.

When finished, he looked up at them with a stunned expression.

"What, John?" Mandy asked.

"He's dropping the case."

Johnny whooped and slapped his hand on the table. Mandy put her face in her hands and wept. John smiled as he turned the letter over and read it all again.

"Here, read it," he said, giving the page to Johnny. "Apparently they had a letter from Joe, saying that he believes the best thing for Christine is to stay with family. And apologizing— *apologizing!*—for bothering them. Can you believe it?"

Johnny was racing through the letter. John was smiling at his wife and she was smiling back at him, nodding, and repeating, "Miracle, miracle."

"Yes," Johnny said. "A miracle. He's got a new engine."

***

He had to call Mike and tell him the good news. And Bill. Bill had told him to ask God for wisdom. And what an answer to prayer he had been given! Bill would be delighted to hear the story of another new engine placed in a dilapidated truck.

With a handful of change, he walked down the road to the pay phone by the saw mill. Inside the booth, he closed the door and scanned the walls, looking for the bright blue card with Mike's phone number on it. He had left it fastened at the center of a jumble of papers and cards, on top of everything else. Someone must have moved it.

But it had not been moved—it had completely disappeared. Johnny riffled through all the lists and cards, but Mike's card was not to be found. He regretted that he had not written down Mike's number and carried it with him. He had no idea how to find or contact the man who had been such a help to him.

"Oh, Mike," he muttered, "I wish I could tell you what's happened."

He did have Bill's card with him, though, and he dialed the home number. Bill answered in his usual hearty way, and was delighted to hear that the caller was Johnny.

Johnny told him the story of the past weekend and the letter the Yoders had received. He explained how he had used Bill's own story of a new engine in showing Joe what God could do in a person's life.

As he talked with Bill, Johnny heard the excitement in his own voice. He realized how *satisfied* he was that he could tell Bill about Joe's transformation. To have been a part of God's work in changing a man's life—that gave him the same feeling that he had when he looked at a full hay mow or a corn crib bursting with a bounty of corn. Except, a hay mow and a corn crib emptied over the winter. A man's soul lived forever.

All that went through his mind as he felt his own excitement rise with the retelling of Joe's story. It *was* Joe and God's story, not Johnny's. God had simply used him to help Joe find the way.

Oh, that's what Audrey meant.

He heard her voice, telling him, "I think of myself as a follower of Jesus Christ, on a mission for Him, and He is using my talents in the circumstances where I find myself." She had said those words with such a serene, peaceful look on her face that Johnny knew she had found the one thing to which she would devote all of her life. He had wondered about it then; now, he felt as though he was beginning to understand.

Bill rejoiced with him.

"He was hungry for hope, Johnny. And there are so many more prodigals out there who feel they are beyond help or redemption. But they still want to hear there *is* hope. And that's why Jesus sends us out with the message," Bill said.

"Did your parents tell you about my job offer?" Bill asked.

"Yes, Bill, but—"

"Wait. Please, hear me out before you make a decision," interrupted Bill.

"All right," Johnny said.

"Our 90 Percent Project is growing beyond anything I ever imagined. We're now sponsoring, consulting on, or initiating projects ourselves in 23 countries, and we have invitations and requests to come to a dozen more.

"We need help, Johnny. I offered you a job once, but you were on another path then, seeking other answers. I'm offering again, but I know I'm talking to a different man now. You've seen what the power of the Gospel can do, in your life and in others. And now you know what it means to be used by God to continue Christ's work on earth—to reach others with God's invitation to come back to Him. You've had a taste of what that work is like, Johnny, and I believe you've found the Gospel to be so powerful that you are feeling a call to missions."

"Bill, this is not something—"

"I know what you're thinking: that you're a farmer and Amish and it's impossible for you to do such a thing. My friend, I hope you know by now that I would never attempt to coerce someone into giving up convictions or commitments. But whenever we talk, I see and hear something in you that tells me God is inviting you to join in His work in this world. He's placed a call on your life, Johnny.

"I know it will turn your life upside down to take this job. I know it will present all kinds of dilemmas for you in your Amish church and lifestyle and—what about your farm? I know how devoted you are to your land. But, Johnny, I feel so strongly led by the Spirit to offer you this job, that I must obey.

"I don't know how everything would work out, but if it's of God, Johnny, then He will be the one working things out. And He's much better at that than either one of us."

Johnny's thoughts were whirling. He said nothing when Bill paused to catch his breath.

"I need someone who knows agriculture and animals. We have so many areas where we could be initiating agricultural projects in tandem with mission work, but right now we have no one who can visit those areas, assess the challenges and potential, and then oversee the projects as they begin and grow. You have the knowledge and the skills we need. Instead of working your own 120 acres, you'd be working in the fields of souls all over the world. The harvest is ready and waiting. The Lord of the harvest wants to send out more workers, and I believe with all my heart that He's calling your name, my friend."

"I'm trying to imagine what I would be saying *yes* to," said Johnny quietly.

"I can tell you several things," Bill answered. "You wouldn't have to live here in Texas, although sometimes we'd need you at headquarters. You really could live anywhere in the country—anywhere in the world, I guess. You would have to have a phone. And, obviously, you'd have to fly. Other than that, my friend, I don't know what all this job will require of you. I do know, though, that you'll be planting and harvesting for eternity."

Johnny listened to it all, stunned. How could Bill think he would even consider such an offer?

Yet, in spite of all his instant, fierce objections, there was another thought that waited quietly for the initial resistance to stop shouting and subside. He was almost afraid to acknowledge that *other* thought, but he knew he must.

Bill knows. He knows exactly how I've been feeling. How could he know?

"Pray about it, Johnny," Bill went on. "Ask God for wisdom and guidance. And we'll talk again. Take your time. After asking God about it, If you feel that you're not being led down this road, then you can say no to me—you *must* say no to me—but at least I've been obedient to what I feel the Spirit is pushing me to do, in opening this door for you.

"I see something in you that is still seeking. Is it possible that God has something more planned for you—something that *you* would never have planned, but God did?

"I think the Heavenly Father has the answers for you, Johnny, if you honestly want to hear Him ..."

Johnny admitted that he had never prayed this way—with his ears open to hearing answers he did not expect or even want.

He felt that old urge to change the subject, to divert the conversation with a joking comment and avoid the questions he did not want to answer.

But, instead, he said, "All right, Bill. I can say yes to that. I will ask God for answers to my questions."

31

Johnny had looked forward to life going back to normal. His sister's wedding was over, and Paul and Naomi were settled in their new home. Audrey had been on his farm—and then had gone. That part of his life was settled. They both knew that anything more than a friendship was impossible. Joe was no longer trying to disrupt Christine's life. Annie's last words to Johnny—about Christine needing something—no longer stalked through his thoughts. Most of all, and most amazing of all, Joe was on a path back to God. And Johnny had been privileged to be a part of God's work in Joe's life.

He had thought, for a few days, that now he need only concentrate on milking, planting, haying, and harvesting. He would tend his animals and his fields, watch the weather, and, as his father had always said, strive to be a good steward of the land.

But the old routine wasn't going to come back. Bill McCollum's words would not permit Johnny to sink back into his old patterns of thought.

"You'll be planting and harvesting for eternity," Bill had said, and Johnny couldn't forget that.

But then, who would be planting and harvesting on his farm? If he, the fourth generation to tend this land, would step away, what would happen to it? His father was already thinking about making a change in jobs. His brother owned the sawmill and was so busy he had hired on four extra people. Besides, Johnny loved this land. He had realized that on his long bicycle trip, when he thought he was headed to a new life. Then he had come to realize that he was a farmer and he had to return to this valley.

But what if that bicycle trip really was leading to a new life? Mike had said that God had plans, and there was no such thing as *coincidence.*

What if God had been guiding his path all along? It was that long ride that had led to his meeting Big Bill, and Samuel, and Audrey. It was on that ride that he had come to the cross Bill had built and had found his own peace through the words written there: "He who has the Son has life." Johnny had claimed those words as words written to reassure him. He stood on those words, knowing now beyond a doubt that his salvation was certain.

And then, his bicycle accident and his meeting with Maureen—was that God working for Dougie's sake? To bring Dougie home safely from the jungles of Viet Nam?

And his meeting with River Man, and his miraculous healing—was it all God working a plan in Johnny's life?

Ever since he had returned from Indiana, Johnny had been convinced that his encounter with Joe had been guided by God, at every turn, in every conversation. But now he was also beginning to suspect that God was also working through that experience to change him, the old Johnny.

He kept thinking about all those people, like Joe, who believed there was no hope for them. How would those people ever hear the same words of assurance he had heard: that God loved them, could change their lives, and would save them forever?

Those few days in Indiana had not only changed Joe—they had also changed Johnny.

Really, though, what could he do to spread the message about Christ? He wasn't a preacher. He certainly didn't think of himself as a missionary. That was just something he would never have thought of doing. Audrey's words came back again. She had said she wasn't a missionary either; God was just using her talents in the situation she found herself.

Couldn't God do that just as easily here, on the farm, in *these* present circumstances? Why would he have to take a job with Bill's mission organization? Realistically, he knew that accepting Bill's proposal would mean he would have to leave the Amish church. He could not balance out what was necessary to do that job with the requirements necessary to be a good member of his church. It wasn't possible.

And then what would happen to life as he knew it? Would his family have to shun him? That was the practice in their church. And John was the bishop of the church. How vividly Johnny remembered his father saying that if he required one thing of his church members, he must require the same of his own family!

His family was the one solid, sure thing Johnny had always counted on. Even when he had gone through his darkest years, when rebellion against the church rules and even against God simmered in his heart, he had always trusted the love and support of his family. He knew he could count on that.

And how would this hurt them? Would it tarnish the respect the community had for his father? Would Mandy be ashamed of her son? Would she feel the sting of the gossip about her son who had, once again, struck out into the world and away from the Amish?

Accepting this job would mean that he would leave behind his farm, his family, and his church. And hurt those people he loved the most.

He tried to pray about his questions, but he felt as if he was talking to the walls. He picked up his Bible, intending to go on reading through the Gospels, but he kept going back to passages he had read in Matthew: Jesus' compassion for lost and hopeless people, His words about coming to heal the sick and set prisoners free, His parables about planting seeds that sometimes took root and flourished and sometimes did not. Johnny read again—and uncomfortably—Jesus' last words to His disciples: "Go into all the world and make disciples, teaching them to observe my commandments."

Go into all the world. Jesus' words. His command.

That was pretty plain, to Johnny's mind. But it just didn't fit with the life he knew.

32

He plodded up the cow path running along the fence, headed up the hill toward the woods. It was Sunday afternoon, and he was restless. He could not read. He could not nap. He did not feel like talking to anyone. He had stepped outside his door to look at the sky and wonder about tomorrow's weather, when he caught a glimpse of the old tree house nestled in the branches of the oak at the edge of the woods.

That tree house had marked milestones in his life. When he was ten, the successful building of that sanctuary had made him feel like a grown man, ready to have his own business and tackle grown-up life. Then the teen years had thrown his life in turmoil, and the tree house was the place he went to think ... and drink, when thinking didn't seem to help him. Still in the tree house were those letters to God he had written in his most desperate times. Still there were the beer bottles that had been transformed by his proposal to Annie. Standing outside his back door, he looked up at the tree house and remembered the Christmas Eve when Annie had said *Yes!,* and how they had sat together and looked out over a glistening, snowy night and dreamed of the future together and Annie had—

Something like an electric shock went through his body. The hair on his arms stood up and he shivered. Annie had said something that night, something that he had not taken too seriously. That night, it had seemed to be only a part of their romantic dreaming.

But now he remembered, and he remembered the look on her face as she had said, *Johnny Miller, you are going to be a strong leader, a wise and kind Christian man that God uses in many ways. I can see it, Johnny! I don't know what troubles or joys lie ahead, but I see God working through you to bring peace and healing to many people.*

What did that mean? He had not thought much about it then and had simply put his arm around her and said, "And you'll be beside me, Annie."

He had been wrong. Annie was no longer beside him. But her words came back. He had not heard her voice for many months, but now he could hear her say those words as clearly as if she were standing behind him.

He shook his head and began walking. He needed a good walk. The old tree house had always been a refuge when he needed to think things through. And a brisk walk up the hill would be good for him, too.

At the base of the oak, he was ready to pull himself up the ladder when he paused, listened, and grinned. He heard the roar of a crowd and an announcer's shrill voice rising over the pandemonium: "It's gone! It's gone! And the Indians have taken the lead ..."

He pulled himself up swiftly, stood up on the deck running around the perimeter of the tree house, and knocked quietly on the door. He heard scrambling inside, papers shuffled, and another noise that sounded like a book falling on the floor. The radio he had heard was silenced.

The door opened slowly and Simon peered out.

"Oh, it's you, Uncle Johnny," said his young nephew.

"Hey, Simon. So, what's the score?"

Simon's face immediately turned a bright pink. He had the same light hair and blue eyes that Johnny had inherited from Mandy. Those blue eyes went, involuntarily, toward the shelf where the radio had been hastily shoved behind a few books.

"I'm kind of surprised the thing still works," said Johnny. "Or isn't it my old one? Maybe you bought a new one of your own?"

Simon's face was going from pink to red. "I had to buy new batteries."

Johnny gave him a grin. "Cheaper than a new radio, at least. So, what's the score?"

"Five to four, and Buddy Bell just hit a three-run homer."

"Wow. Is he having a good year? I've kind of lost track of what the Indians are doing."

Simon was beginning to relax.

"He's one of my favorites. I think he's going to be one of their greatest third basemen, ever!"

"Well, don't let me keep you from any exciting plays," said Johnny. "I just thought I'd come up and look around a bit." He had been up to the tree house just a few weeks before, when Bill had asked to see it, but he didn't mention that to Simon.

Simon looked a little anxious.

"It's okay if I use the tree house, isn't it?"

"Sure, Simon. Help yourself. I built it when I was your age, and now I have other things to keep me busy. But if it's going to be your hideaway, maybe I should move some of my things out of here. You can bring up whatever you want to make the place yours."

Johnny was looking around. The beer bottles must go. He didn't know if Simon was following in his footsteps concerning the beer, but he hoped not. His old books and magazines were still there, along with his notebooks where he had many notes and sketches on leaves, flowers, birds, and butterflies. Animals, though, had always been harder to sketch, he mused. *I never was very good at animals.*

His eyes rested on the note he had stuck on a nail the night he had given up trying to sort out everything in his life and decided, instead, to let Jesus guide him. He had written, *Tonight my prayers were answered. Jesus gave me a new life. I am a new creature. And I am going to follow Jesus.*

He walked over to the wall and gently wiggled the paper off the nail, then stood reading it again.

"What does that mean, Uncle Johnny?"

"What does what mean? This paper?"

"The words. What happened? Why did you write that?"

Johnny's blue eyes met his nephew's. The boy seemed so young, and the story behind that paper seemed so big and complex—what would Simon understand? How much should he say?

"I wrote this the night I realized that the only way to find real life is to let God give me a new life. We become new people when we let God into our lives. That's really the most important thing in the world, Simon. And Jesus helps us live out that new life."

"Is that what following Jesus means?"

"Yes. Following His commands. Living the way He taught. Doing what He asks us to do …"

Johnny felt a lump rising in his throat.

Simon's eyes widened as he gazed at his uncle's face

"Uncle Johnny, are you crying?" he asked.

Johnny grinned. It was true, his eyes were full.

"Well," he said briskly. "There's crying. And there's crying. There's lots of kinds of crying, Simon."

Simon frowned.

"You'll find out, as you grow older," Johnny said, still grinning and blinking rapidly. "Look, I'll take some of these things with me now, and I'll clean out more in the next week or two. Then you can do whatever you want with this place. How does that sound?"

"Thanks, Uncle Johnny!" Simon was delighted.

Johnny folded the paper carefully and slid it into his pocket. He cleared the books, magazines, and newspapers off one shelf. The radio stood there, exposed and alone.

"Leave the radio?" Johnny asked, looking at Simon.

The youngster's blue eyes danced.

"Yes!"

***

He carried the armload of his old treasures down the hill. The farm lay below him, peaceful and quiet on a Sunday afternoon. There was no traffic on the county road. His summer world seemed to be resting and waiting, preparing itself for tomorrow.

He had walked that path so many times, he had no need to think about walking it. Instead, his mind was on words he had written years before. *Jesus gave me a new life.*

It reminded him of words Jesus had spoken and Matthew had recorded. He couldn't remember the exact wording, but Jesus had said, "Whoever wants to save his life will lose it. But whoever loses his life for me will find it."

What did that mean for Johnny? Right now?

Was it impossible for him to hold onto life as he knew it—even as he might have wanted it to be—if he was going to follow Jesus?

I just told Simon that following Jesus means doing what He asks us to do. Is Jesus asking me to turn my life upside down?

In the kitchen, he dropped the books and papers on the table and went to the living room, where he sat down in Annie's chair. It had become his chair. His Bible lay open on the stand next to it. He picked up the Bible and turned once again to the book of Matthew.

Where was that?

Oh, yes. Chapter 4.

It was the story about Jesus calling several of His disciples. He was walking along the lake, saw two brothers who were fishermen, and said to them, "Come, follow me, and I'll show you how to fish for people."

And they did. Just like that. They left everything behind—their boat, their nets, their father (who was in the business with them), and their partners. Those men left their old lives behind. They had families, too. There surely were consequences of their decisions to follow Jesus. Surely their decision shook their families and their communities.

If following Jesus meant Johnny had to take this job with Bill, then there would be consequences, in his family, his church, and his own life. Johnny felt a physical ache in his chest as he imagined what would happen to the Miller family if he said yes to Bill.

Then he thought about Joe. He remembered the bitterness and despair he had first heard in John Miller's voice. He remembered the hopelessness that had gripped the man. And he could picture the look on Joe's face that Sunday morning when he was enveloped by his cousin's embrace.

If Johnny forgot about all that, pushed it back into memory as a one-time incident, and convinced himself God was asking nothing more of him—then what might the eternal consequences be?

He raised his eyes. His glance fell on his two walking sticks. He had moved them to a corner of the living room because everyone kept knocking them over when they were behind the kitchen door. Now he gazed at the mesquite stick, the one that had started out rough and awkward, but had been smoothed and polished by River Man's knife. Johnny had applied a finish to it that had heightened the beauty of the grain and the carvings. On the stick, River Man had carved a cross, and at the base of the cross was a sheaf of wheat. Resting on the sheaf was a butterfly.

Without the cross, where would he be now? Johnny realized that the cross was the turning point for everyone—coming to the cross, being cleansed and transformed by Christ's love and His power. The butterfly symbolized the transformation; Johnny remembered telling River Man about how God had transformed both him and Annie.

And the sheaf of wheat?

He heard Jesus' words, slightly altered for his ears.

Come, follow me, Johnny, and I'll show you how to plant seeds that bring an eternal harvest.

33

He awoke. Again. Rolling over, he looked at the softly glowing numbers on the face of the Big Ben alarm clock. 2:34. He had slept less than an hour. All night he had been dozing, waking to wrangle stampeding thoughts and emotions, then dozing, and waking.

He sighed and dropped his legs over the edge of the bed.

But instead of rising, he sat there for a full five minutes.

What was the best way to start? Perhaps he should start by explaining the turmoil in his head and soul the last few days? How could he ever describe that? Should he open the conversation by telling them how thankful he was for his parents, his family, the way he had been raised? Or should he plunge right in with an apology, *I know this is going to be hard for you. I'm sorry for what it will put you through.*

He lay back down on the bed and pulled the quilt up around his shoulders. Mandy had made the quilt; she had started piecing it the same week Annie had come back from that trip to Indiana to talk with Joe. Even though Johnny had not yet proposed to Annie, Mandy declared later that she had known then, when Johnny and Annie returned from Indiana, that they would someday need a quilt to cover *their* bed.

He had certainly not given his parents an easy road in their raising of their youngest son. The wandering, the drinking, the

long battle with questions and doubt as he grieved losing Annie—
all of those must have been so hard on his parents. Even as a young
boy, he had been ornery and willful. Sly and sneaky sometimes,
too. He could see all that, looking back.

And now, he was about to deal them a blow he wished with all
his heart he could spare them. But there was no other way.

***

During milking, he was unusually quiet. As he relieved the
cows of their burden, he caressed the warm hides and murmured
words of affection. He squirted twice as many streams of milk to
the waiting cat. Finished with the chores, he lingered at the barn
door, taking a long look, as though he was storing away memories
and thinking he might never set foot there again.

He had little to say at breakfast. Mandy and John talked
quietly about their plans for the day. Every now and then, Mandy
glanced at Johnny, who seemed too absorbed in his thoughts to eat,
then at John, with that questioning look that the family understood
as well as spoken words. John directed a question at his son one
time and, not receiving an answer, had to repeat it a bit more
firmly.

Mandy and John had finished eating. Johnny was simply
fingering his coffee cup and staring at the stove. His eggs were still
on his plate. Cold.

John pushed back his chair.

"Well—" he said.

Finally, after a long, restless night of trying to craft the perfect
approach to his announcement, Johnny simply blurted it out:

"I have to tell Bill I'll take the job."

Mandy's eyes went immediately to her husband's face. The
two men were looking at each other gravely. She got up and
collected a few dishes to take to the sink. Johnny's eyes were still

on his father's face, but his peripheral vision caught a sense of tightness in his mother's countenance.

"I've been praying for God's guidance and wisdom for you, son," said John finally and slowly. "And for us. I think we've known for a long time that this day would come. At least, your mother says she has known. I suppose I knew, too, but wanted to ignore the signs."

"I am not leaving the Amish, Dad," said Johnny, leaning forward and even—he shocked himself—with a slight smile on his face. "I am not leaving *you*. I am following Jesus. When I first chose to let Christ lead me through life, all I wanted was to have Him solve my problems. I had made such a mess of things. He was the only hope I had as an answer to my problems. But I made a promise that day that I would follow Him.

"I never expected this; I thought my promise meant I would just have to change my bad habits and try to live a good life—but now it's become so much more for me. He gave me a new life; I never would have had it without Him. I never thought He'd ask me to move out of this valley, but now He has. There's something more He wants me to do.

"I have prayed and prayed about this, and I believe it is God's will for me to take this job. I feel almost like the disciples must have felt when Jesus called them—torn between two good things, but knowing that if He calls, then I am going to go. I must go."

As he heard himself say the words, he realized, with a start, that Annie had written something similar to him the night of her accident, as she battled pain and fought off unconsciousness to write the words to her husband: *I do love you with all my heart, but I love Jesus more. If He calls, I must go.*

Those words had stung, and they tormented him for months. He knew, of course, that Annie must love God first. That was the way things *should* be—but that didn't ease the hurt of her leaving him because she loved Someone else more. Now he understood what she had written. He loved his family and his farm and this way of life dearly; but Jesus had spoken directly to him, had said, *Come, follow me, Johnny, and I'll show you how to plant seeds that bring an eternal harvest,* and he knew he would have no peace until he followed.

John nodded slowly, tugging at his beard, his eyes still holding his son's.

Mandy turned from the sink and walked over to stand beside her husband, laying a gentle hand on his shoulder. Johnny could see the streak of one tear on her right cheek. He felt guilt rising up, attempting to throttle his determination.

"But what this will put you through ... I'm sorry. I wish—"

"Son, there are always consequences when difficult choices are made. We will deal with whatever comes," interrupted his father. "Our highest prayer has always been that our children would grow into Godly people, and if this is the way God is guiding you, then so be it."

John glanced up at Mandy, then placed his hand over hers, still on his shoulder. "We made the decision to stay in the Amish church because we believed this was the best way to bring up our children in the way they should go. And when we made that decision, we caused pain, too. Your mother lost her best friend."

This was something Johnny had never known.

"Mom?" He took his eyes off his dad's face to look at his mother. She nodded.

"Esther and I grew up together. While we were both dating, she and her boyfriend were planning to leave the Amish, and your dad and I had talked about it, too; but we made the choice to stay because, as Dad says, we were convinced that this was the best way for our family to live. When we made that choice, Esther thought I was condemning her, that I believed I was better than her because we were staying in the church and she was—well, she used the word *wicked.* I never wanted to lose her friendship; she was closer to me than my sisters. But she drifted away." Johnny was surprised to see his mother's eyes fill again. "I still miss her sometimes."

"We have always told you, son, that the church doesn't save you. Only Jesus can do that," said John. He was looking at Johnny with an expression that Johnny had never seen on his father's face. Johnny couldn't quite put a word to it, but it somehow made him feel ... stronger.

"What *does* this mean for you, Johnny?" asked his mother quietly.

"I don't know exactly. Even Bill couldn't tell me the details of what all I might be doing. I know I'll be traveling. I'll have to use a phone. I expect I'll be in Texas some of the time. I suppose—" For the first time, his voice broke. "I suppose I can't continue to farm this place. And I don't know where I'll live."

He had barely finished before Mandy's words came rushing out.

"You'll live here. You might be traveling a lot, but your house—your home—will always be here."

Johnny looked at his dad. "You won't be allowed to do that."

Mandy answered. "Things are changing. Maybe it's time we changed some of our practices. I never could understand tearing families apart..." she stopped suddenly, with a glance at her husband. John remained silent.

"It would go against church rules," said Johnny firmly, "and I don't want to put you in that position."

"We'll pray for wisdom and deal with things as they come," John repeated. "And, son, man-made rules must never stand in the way of someone following Jesus."

34

Johnny wanted to tell Paul and Naomi before the news somehow drifted on the wind over to their church district. They were his two best friends; Paul, the boy with whom he had grown up, double-dated, and shared adventures, trouble, and dreams. Naomi was the closest sibling he had. She knew him better than anyone else in his family knew him. He grinned to himself as he thought about her. *She even knows things about me that I would never tell her!*

Yes, he wanted to be the one to tell them about this decision.

Later that afternoon, he hitched Joyce to the road cart and drove the six miles to their home. He wanted to time his visit so that Paul would be home from his job on the construction crew. On these summer days, the crew started before daybreak and ended their days early.

Joyce trotted into the driveway of the little cottage and stopped by the hitching rail at the barn. The newlyweds were renting a small house with a barn but had only an acre or so of pasture for the horse and a small garden plot.

"Johnny!" Naomi's face lit up when he opened her kitchen door and stepped inside. "Oh, I thought maybe it was Paul. He'll be happy to see you; he just mentioned last night that he hasn't talked to you since the wedding. Come in, come in. How about some pie and coffee?" Her kitchen was very warm and was filled with the aroma of fresh bread.

"It's too hot for coffee," he answered. "How about some iced tea? Got any of that? Is Paul home yet?"

"Any minute now," his sister answered cheerily. He could not miss the sparkle in her eye as she thought of her new husband coming home.

And within two minutes, a pickup truck pulled into the driveway and dropped off a tired, dirty Paul. Naomi and Johnny called to him from their chairs on the porch. Paul sat down beside them, and Johnny again noticed the tenderness between the two, although only a few words of greeting were spoken. For just a moment, he felt, strangely, like a lonely outsider.

"Good to see you, Johnny. What brings you over here?" asked Paul.

He told them about Big Bill's offer. About the conflict it had triggered within his head and heart. About the words of Scripture that kept coming back to him. And he even told them about the words he had heard from Jesus. They listened without interrupting.

When he finished, no one spoke for several minutes. At one time, it would have been his nature to rush into the silence and defend, argue, or explain himself. Instead, he waited.

Paul spoke first.

"You've had quite a decision to make, but I believe God has led you. So we will support you in whatever way we can."

Such a simple response, but it was everything he had hoped for. They, too, might be bound by church rules as Johnny went forward with whatever God had planned, but they, too, would deal with the consequences in whatever way they could. *In the end,* Johnny thought, *everything is in God's hands.* That thought gave him great peace.

"Will you be moving?" asked Naomi.

"I don't know yet what will happen. I'll have to make some arrangements with the farm. I don't think Dad can handle it alone—I know he doesn't want to—and he might even decide to take another job with Bill and won't be able to do the farm work. I certainly can't leave or move until that's straightened out."

Naomi looked at her husband and grinned. It was obvious they had some secret between them.

"Well," said Paul, smiling at his wife but speaking to Johnny, "we have some news for you, too. We've been talking a lot about our future." His gaze shifted back to Johnny. "We always knew this house was only a temporary place, to give us a start, until we settled on what we wanted to do. But now that we're married and it's our hope there will be a family before too long, I would really like to get back to farming. I've been working on construction ever since I was old enough to work away from home, but as a husband and dad, I want to be home and working with my family. I don't want to be going off every day, sometimes leaving at two in the morning for distant jobs. We've been talking about looking for farmland. And now you have come with this news …"

Johnny was stunned. He had never expected this—and he couldn't have planned it any better himself.

It was the perfect answer—for all of them.

**

Mandy was adamant. Even if he was absent for long periods of time, the little house would be kept as it was—Johnny's home. Within a week, Paul and Naomi, in great excitement, had chosen an acre of land just across Strawberry Lane on which they would build their own home. Johnny would stay through the summer, helping Paul settle in as steward of the Miller family land. And even when Johnny was gone, his father would be there to advise Paul.

Within a month, the news came, too, that Paul and Naomi would indeed have a family to fill their new home. By next summer, there would be a new baby in the family.

The farm was alive with activity and the sense of change. Great piles of dirt were moved as the basement for the new house was dug and the blocks laid up. Paul's crew was working on the house, and although they were also busy with other projects elsewhere, they were experienced and well-organized and they responded to Paul's urgency. The house was under roof by mid-summer.

Paul was working on both the house and the farm, and sometimes he was in the fields late at night. Still, he always made the trip home, although he was offered a bed in the big farmhouse.

It was good, for that summer, for Johnny to work side by side with his friend and brother-in-law. Naomi was often over, too, and Johnny felt the sense that "his" farm was slowly making the shift to becoming "their" farm.

But that was good. It was as it should be. Johnny's eyes were now on another horizon, on other fields to be planted. God had once again changed his heart and he felt himself slowly loosening his grasp on what he had once thought would be his life. There was another, new life waiting for him. God was giving him a peace about letting go of the old and following Jesus into something new. Sometimes, when he stopped to think about how all the details were falling into place so that he could transition into that new life, he marveled—and gave thanks.

True, the unknowns of the new life sometimes caused him some hesitation. There was, for example, the day he first stepped onto an airplane.

Bill McCollum, too, had started his construction project that summer. John had decided to decline Bill's offer of a job managing the new factory, but at least once a week, Bill's big Stetson sat on the shelf inside Mandy's kitchen door, lined up with the Millers' and Paul's straw hats. He was a regular guest at their supper table (or sometimes lunch), and he would sit talking with John, seeking advice on doing business in this new area.

Josh Richardson usually piloted Bill's private jet to Ohio. For the first few trips, they flew into Columbus and then rented a car to drive up to Milford because neither the small airport in Stevenson nor any of the surrounding county had car-rental services. Finally, Bill found a three-bedroom house for rent close to Stevenson. He bought an older model car at the used-car lot in town, and set up the rental house for use whenever he and any of his personnel came to town on business. Josh and the private jet became well known and well liked at the Stevenson airport.

The day came when Bill decided it was time for Johnny to fly. He came to lunch that day and then whisked Johnny off to the airport. They were going to fly to Texas. Johnny wasn't sure which emotion was stronger—excitement or apprehension. Bill grinned at him as they strapped themselves into their seats.

"Nervous?"

"Sure. A bit."

"It's nothing like riding in a buggy, I can tell you that. But it does have some advantages. We couldn't do what we do without being able to fly."

No, it was nothing like rattling along behind Joyce's rump. Johnny's stomach quivered, and he felt a strange sensation in his ears—as though the powerful force of the plane blasting upward into the sky had also broken apart something inside his head. Bill assured him the "popping" was normal and he would get used to it, but Johnny wasn't sure that was a "normal" he would like. And his eyes played tricks on his brain—the hills below them flattened out as the plane rose!

It was a clear day, and he was fascinated by the patchwork of fields, cities, lakes, rivers, forests, and highways that passed below him. Flying high above all earthbound highways, there were no signs or landmarks to indicate where they were. Bill, however, seemed familiar with the route. He would say, "Take a look at that city. That's St. Louis, and there's the Mississippi," or, "We're over Texas now." Johnny had never seen the earth from this perspective; but the thought of being suspended so high in the air did make him a bit uneasy.

Back on the ground once again, at the airport in Laredo, Johnny's knees were steady enough to walk down the steps of the plane and through the hangar to a parking area. He immediately spotted Bill's old, battered pickup waiting for them.

"Still driving that thing." It was a statement, not a question.

"Yup. Engine's good as new," said Bill as they climbed in. He looked over at Johnny, grinned, and gave a thumbs-up.

35

Johnny had only been in Texas a few days, but when Bill drove him back to the farm, he looked at his valley with new eyes, as though he had been absent a long time. It *looked* different. Paul and Naomi's house was already blending into the landscape, as though it had been there for years; the corn must be at least a foot higher; and Joyce—he mused sadly to himself as he brushed down the horse the next day—Joyce was beginning to show her age. She moved more slowly, as though her knees were stiffening up. He'd have to call the vet and have him take a look at the horse.

And, somehow, Johnny had stepped outside the whole picture. He felt strangely detached from the farm, the fields, the coming harvest, and even life here in the valley. He would stay to help Paul through the next few months, but this was no longer the center of his life. It was a bit unsettling, because he had not yet found another center, other than his determination to follow wherever God might lead him next. At the same time, he felt a deep peace with that decision to wait on God to shine light on the next step.

In Texas, Bill had shown Johnny around the 90 Percent Project offices and introduced him to people with whom he'd soon be working. He had met Bill's wife, Penny, and had supper at their house one night. At times, he was aware of the curious scrutiny of folks who must have never seen an Amish man before. He had considered buying other clothes for these first meetings. Then he had also recollected how, in the first hours of his bicycle trip, he had been so eager to don blue jeans and to shave and wash Amish down the drain. But now, he felt no urgency in shedding his Amish appearance; in fact, he acknowledged that he was quite reluctant to do so.

He came home laden with files, maps, and proposals for projects that Bill wanted him to study. Visits to certain areas would come later.

The day they arrived back in Ohio, Naomi had cooked a supper in the big farmhouse and carried it across Strawberry Lane to feed the crew who was working late on the new house.

"Come on over," she called to Bill and Johnny. She was walking across the lawn, carrying what looked like a pot of soup, as the two men walked up the sidewalk to Johnny's house. "There's plenty."

Bill looked undecided.

"Sure, stay," said Johnny. "She said there's plenty. And nobody makes bread like Naomi."

So Johnny and Bill joined the crew for supper, served on a makeshift table in Paul and Naomi's new house. Afterward, the two of them sat on five-gallon buckets on the long front porch, both quiet for a while, pondering their own thoughts as they relaxed amid sounds of hammers punctuating the quiet of the summer evening.

"I thought Texas went well," Bill finally began. "What did you think of it all?"

"To be honest, my head is so full of everything I've seen and heard that I don't know what I'm thinking right now."

Bill chuckled.

"I can understand that. We'll just take one step at a time. It looks like things are working out here."

"Yes, and, surprisingly, I feel good about all this change. On the day I called to tell you I'd take the job, I thought to myself that I'd never before experienced such a peace. I know the way is not going to be smooth, but I am convinced that God has been leading me down this path—for years. And He's been putting everything in place, at just the right time. It gives me reassurance that I've made the right decision. It also reminds me of that verse in Scripture that talks about God going before us. Preparing our way, so to speak." Johnny paused, and then went on. "And He's doing the same for Paul and Naomi. I watch them this summer, I see how excited and content they are …"

He let the sentence hang. Bill shifted on the makeshift stool that was becoming uncomfortable and gave Johnny a sideways glance.

"Is *everything* coming together for you?"

Johnny looked at him, puzzled.

"What do you mean?"

"I'll just speak my mind, straight out. What about you and Audrey? At the beginning of the summer, I would have said that by now you two would be together."

The name, spoken aloud, hit Johnny's heart at some unguarded spot.

He stared at the new wood of the porch floor and found himself gently tugging on his beard.

He decided not to dance around the question.

"I watch Naomi and Paul begin their life together here, and I am truly happy for them. But, yes, it also makes me wonder if there will ever be a wife and family for me. Maybe not. As for Audrey—well, I think we pretty well closed the door on that when she was here for the wedding."

"Hmm. I wouldn't be too sure of that, my friend." Johnny was still studying the grain of the wood in the floor, but he could tell Bill was grinning. "At your sister's wedding last spring, it was pretty obvious how you two felt about each other. You two are so well suited to each other. Oh, my wife would love to hear me now—playing Cupid. I generally like to stay out of these things. But you, my friend, need to have your eyes opened."

Johnny looked at Bill.

"She'd never leave the orphanage. That's her life."

"Maybe. But maybe not her *complete* life. Maybe God has more for you both." Bill stood up and stretched. "There's only one way for you to find out."

"I can't see how we could make that work. She wants to be in Mexico. I'll be traveling."

Bill's deep, hearty laugh burst out.

"Would you ever have imagined all that God has done in your life? All this?" His arm swept in an arc, taking in the fields and the houses. "And then all He is going to be doing in worldwide harvest fields? Would you ever have thought all this could happen in your life?" Bill leaned on the porch railing, looking out over the valley.

Johnny smiled. "No, sir," he said, shaking his head. "No, I would never have imagined all this could happen."

"Young man, look at what God has already done in your life. He can handle those little details like your home address. Give Him a chance with your heart, too!"

36

The summer moved into September, Paul and Naomi moved into their new home, and every day that passed moved Johnny one step closer to his new life.

When he stopped to think about everything that had happened over the past five years of his life, he began to see that Jesus had been calling him for some time; he had just not had ears that heard. But even though he had not heard clearly, Jesus had been teaching him, preparing him for this new path.

Bill had implied that Audrey was also part of the path God had chosen for Johnny, but Johnny couldn't quite see that. Sometimes his mind went back to the conversation with Bill on Naomi's front porch, and he found himself wondering ... After all, with Audrey, he had felt ...

But no, it was impossible. He would slam the door shut, not allowing such thoughts to parade around in his head. There might be someone else, someday. He might eventually find for himself a love like the love Paul and Naomi shared. But it wouldn't be with Audrey. It couldn't be with Audrey.

There. He had it settled. He would wait for *someone.*

But then, he would catch an intimate glance between Paul and Naomi or hear the affection in their voices as they talked, and see

Naomi's quiet excitement whenever her baby was mentioned—and his thoughts went immediately to Audrey.

No. It could not be.

Thus, he was quite taken aback—and uncomfortable—when Audrey's name again came up.

Paul was still working, in the evenings, on finishing the interior of the house. They were living in the basement, and there was still plenty of work to be done before the upstairs would be used as the main level of the home. The next day, Johnny would be leaving for another short trip to Texas, and he had told Paul he'd be over to discuss plans for the coming week on the farm.

Johnny was just crossing Strawberry Lane when Naomi called from her front door.

"Johnny! Could you please bring the mail up?"

He stopped at their mailbox and withdrew a stack of envelopes. A jolt went through him when he saw the stamp and return address on one of them—a letter from Audrey.

Of course, he knew Audrey and his sister had been corresponding regularly, ever since they had met in his hospital room in Texas. It was just that now, when he was trying *not* to think about Audrey—there was her name, and her handwriting … in his hand.

Equally unsettling was something else from Mexico, a newsletter from the orphanage. It was a simple brochure, without an envelope. He could see and read part of the first page. He would never read Naomi's private mail, but this was, well, not private.

On the front page were children's drawings of beautiful, brilliant Monarch butterflies. Audrey had written the text underneath the photo. The migrating butterflies would be returning to the Michoacan mountains in about two months. Their return coincided with the corn harvest and many local festivals. Audrey was writing about it to describe the festivities the children of the orphanage had planned.

He could hear her voice.

Come see the butterflies sometime, Johnny. But don't bring the bicycle.

He realized he was standing at Paul and Naomi's mailbox, reading their mail. He hurried up to the house.

Naomi was putting away the last of the washed supper dishes. He heard Paul's footsteps upstairs, and then a few quick strikes of a hammer.

Hoping his sister hadn't seen him reading their mail, Johnny laid the stack on the table, careful to put Audrey's letter under other envelopes so that her handwriting wouldn't be staring up at him. But Naomi immediately picked up the bundle and shuffled through it.

"Oh, a letter from Audrey," she said, with great pleasure.

"I'll go see Paul," Johnny mumbled, turning toward the stairs.

"Johnny."

Johnny thought that Naomi sounded exactly like Mandy as she said his name and commanded him to stop.

He turned and waited. He knew his sister. He knew what she was going to say.

"Johnny, isn't it time you wrote to Audrey?"

"I can't see a reason ..."

"Johnny!"

He knew that tone, too. His sister was a bit exasperated with him.

"When Audrey was here for the wedding, everybody knew she was interested in you—more than interested. It was obvious something was there, between you two. But you had closed the door. She asked me for advice, but all I could say was that you had made your choice. I couldn't encourage her to do or say anything that would work against what you had decided was best. I wanted to, though. But it wouldn't have been right.

"Now you have made another decision, and your life is

changing. Things are different than they were back in the spring. Johnny, I know you two care about each other. She asks about you in every letter. And I can see it in you; when she was here, and every time her name comes up—you care about her, too. When are you going to admit it and write to her?"

"I wasn't planning—"

"Maybe not. But don't you think you should?"

He had rarely heard his sister be so ... *bossy.* That was the word that came to mind. A grin almost broke through his beard, but his discomfort with this conversation squelched the humor. He might as well be honest with Naomi; she could always read his thoughts, anyway.

"I don't know. I just don't know what to do. I don't see how we could make a marriage work."

"You love each other. You both want to follow God's leading." Naomi's voice softened a bit. "Why not?

"Johnny, you do love her, don't you?"

Johnny felt his neck getting warm. He let his gaze go to the scene outside the window.

"I ... I think so."

Naomi would not let him avoid it any longer.

"You *think* so? You *know* so! Don't you?"

She had him. She had always known. His little sister was like that.

"All right, yes, I love her. Yes. I do."

"Then, my dear brother, go get her!"

37

The violent trembling had quieted, and the thin body only gave a shiver now and then as the child huddled in her arms. Audrey held him close and kept rocking.

She loved this little village, the mountain views, and the people who had made her a part of their community, and she would never trade this place for the streets and businesses of Malibu. But she would trade any treasure she had if she could only have a doctor here.

The frail five-year-old in her arms had been brought to them just three weeks before by the priest who traveled from town to town. He had found the boy on a deserted mountain road, frightened and hungry. The boy would not speak to the priest; he would not speak to anyone at the orphanage either.

Gradually, he had begun to join in the play of the children and he sat quietly during school hours, watching, listening, and sometimes joining in whatever activity he could. But there were times when the violent trembling began, and then Audrey would gather him up in her arms and hold him close until the shaking subsided and he was left exhausted and, she thought as she looked into his eyes, sad.

She was fairly certain these were not epileptic seizures. Some emotional trigger brought them on, but she had not yet detected what it was that sparked such episodes.

Still, she wished a doctor could check the boy, just to be certain. She had talked with her mother about the possibility of finding a doctor for the village, but the only thing her mother could promise was that she would see that a doctor visited sometime in the next month. But that was only one visit. As for the hope of any medical professional becoming a resident here—well, that was something the board would have to work on. Audrey knew that process would take a while, maybe even years.

Her thoughts had wandered away from her classroom, but she smiled when she realized the little one had reached up and twined the end of her ponytail around his fingers. She was the only light-haired person in the village, and everyone, adults included, regarded her hair with awe. *And it's not even "light,"* she thought. To her eyes, her hair was an ordinary, medium brown, with shades of red. Still, it seemed to amaze her children and neighbors here.

She planted a soft kiss on the small brown forehead and began to unfold him from her arms. Carmella, her assistant, was reading a book to the other children seated in a circle around her at the far corner of the room.

The younger children would soon be dismissed. Carmella was twelve, and she was also in the older class that had their studies in the morning, but Carmella was determined to be a teacher like Miss Audrey, and so Audrey had named the girl the official "teacher's aide" for the younger class. Audrey knew that several young men in the village had their eye on Carmella, but Audrey would hear nothing of an early marriage for this girl. It might be acceptable in this village's culture, but Audrey was determined to forestall it. Yet she knew that a decision would soon have to be made about the girl's future.

The thought of marriages brought Naomi to mind. Her letters had been filled with the excitement of a new marriage, a new house, and a new baby. Lately, though, Naomi had written nothing about Johnny …

Audrey forced her thoughts back to her schoolroom.

She took the little boy by the hand and led him back to the circle gathered around Carmella. Obediently, he sat down, but his eyes stayed on Audrey. She smiled at him with reassurance in her eyes until he smiled back, and then she turned to her desk while Carmella kept on reading.

It's a glorious day out there, she thought as she glanced out the window. The windows were open, and the air smelled of autumn. The sky was a turquoise blue, unbroken by clouds. From the second-story window, she could see the entire village, no more than twenty houses, now basking in the sunshine. People were finding excuses to be outside, puttering in their yards, visiting with neighbors, enjoying the perfect weather. The rainy season was over, and the one main road in town had finally dried out.

What? Who is that?

She leaned into the open window. Far down the road, a straw hat moved along at a steady, determined pace. It was different from all the other hats in the village. And she recognized that gait.

"Johnny!"

Startled, the children stared at their teacher. She had never before shouted like that in class. And now she was leaning halfway out the window!

"Carmella, watch the children," said Audrey breathlessly, and without waiting for an answer, she ran out of the room, down the stairs, and into the road.

He was walking along, taking in everything around him, but he had not seen her yet. On ground level, she stopped and took in the unbelievable sight of Johnny Miller in her village. His beard.

His blue denim pants and suspenders. His coat, clutched in his left hand.

Dear Johnny! You are here!

She stopped, watching him for a moment, saying to herself, *He is here. He is really here.*

He bent over to pat a dog that had trotted up to greet him.

The old lady who lived next door and sat all day on a rickety chair on her stoop called to Audrey. Without looking at her, Audrey called a good afternoon back.

Johnny heard her voice and stood up, looking around. *Looking for her.*

He saw her then, and a grin broke through his beard.

That heart-stopping grin.

She didn't know whether she was going to laugh or cry.

He resumed walking, twice as fast now. In a moment, he was standing in front of her, still grinning.

She grabbed him in a fierce hug. Immediately, she felt the tension in his body and remembered. *He wouldn't do this ...*

She began to draw back, but then *he* was returning the embrace.

They both began talking at once.

"What are you doing here?"

"Naomi sent me. You know how sisters are—"

Then Audrey did draw back.

"Naomi sent you?"

"She understands me better than I do myself. I couldn't ... I didn't ... Oh, I'll try to explain it," Johnny began quickly. He glanced around. "Is this where you live?"

Audrey was suddenly aware of the old lady leaning forward in her chair, trying to see and hear everything. She glanced past Johnny. It seemed everyone in the village had suddenly found a reason to be outside, with faces turned toward their schoolteacher and the stranger who had walked into town.

"Come. I still have a class upstairs. But it's time to dismiss them." She turned toward the orphanage, looking upward toward the window, and saw the opening full of little heads, all straining to see what was happening. Carmella stood behind them.

Audrey led Johnny into the orphanage and up the stairs. She was smiling so broadly that she could hardly speak. She even felt like *giggling.*

"Children, my friend Johnny has come for a visit. Class is over for today," she said.

The children had scrambled back to their seats when they heard the footsteps on the stairs, but now they jumped up and began to leave the classroom.

"Do you want me to put things away, Miss Audrey?" asked Carmella. Audrey saw the admiration shining in the girl's eyes as she glanced shyly at Johnny. Carmella had seen the greeting on the road. Audrey was sure her young mind was busy concocting romance.

"No, thank you, Carmella. I'll take care of it later."

Carmella left, with one last curious glance toward Johnny.

"I didn't understand any of that," said Johnny. "It's been a strange experience, being in a world where you don't understand most of what's being spoken around you."

"Yes, I imagine so," said Audrey, not thinking about what she was saying but gazing into those blue eyes, trying to read what was there.

"Now," she said, "what's this about Naomi sending you? Why would she send you here?"

"She said it was time I came to get you."

Audrey felt herself flushing. She realized she was holding her breath. *What was he saying?*

"I asked her not to tell you I was coming," Johnny continued. "I hope she didn't?"

"No, she never gave a hint. She writes about her new house

and the baby and that they're on the farm now. Johnny! What made them decide to move to the farm? What's going on?"

"It's a long story," he said. "It might take me a long time to tell you everything."

"We have two hours until supper. Here, sit down. Tell me."

"No," he replied with a grin and a look in his eye that melted her. "No, I meant it might take *years.*"

38

Audrey did not have her own house. Not even an apartment. That would have been a luxury beyond this little village. She did have her own room at the orphanage and had created a sanctuary for herself behind the building.

They stopped at the director's house next door and Audrey poked her head in the kitchen door to tell the director's wife that there would be another person for supper. Then she and Johnny went to her sanctuary.

Between the steep, wooded mountainside rising behind the village and the orphanage building, Audrey had found a spot half hidden by five-foot flowering bushes. In the semicircle created by the bushes and rocks of the mountain, she had placed a chair, a small crate she used as a table, a bird bath, several bird feeders, and pots that had been brilliant with color in the summer but now held only the drooping, shriveled remains of their former glory. Sitting in her sanctuary, Audrey felt removed from the rest of the village. The children had learned that she went there to read and pray and rest, and so they rarely intruded or disturbed her.

Audrey motioned for Johnny to take the chair, but he insisted she do so, and he found a spot on a large, flat rock. They could hear the voices of the playing children and dogs barking and people sometimes calling to each other, but they were in their own world. Every now and then, a small head peered around the hedge to take a look at Teacher and the stranger and then quickly drew back again.

"Tell me everything that's happened." Audrey leaned forward, her elbows on her knees, hugging herself. Johnny was close enough to her that she wanted to reach out and take his hand or touch his arm, but she knew she could not.

"So much has happened. It's been quite a summer. But I do want to tell you everything," said Johnny.

This was a new Johnny who had come to her. He was not hesitant or confused or guarded. She could not stop smiling.

"Then where shall we start?" She didn't want to ask, but it seemed the natural question: "Did you come to see the butterflies?"

"Butterflies?" He was puzzled for a moment, then she saw that he understood. "Oh, I forgot about the butterflies. They're due in Mexico soon, aren't they?"

She nodded. "This week or next."

"No, not the butterflies," he said firmly. "I came to see you."

She couldn't help herself. Her smile grew even wider, and she beamed at him.

"I'm glad. It's so good to see you."

"I'm wondering … I know you love these children and teaching here. I can already see that they love you. You've said you want to change one little life at a time. But what if you could change hundreds of lives next year? What if you set your sights beyond this mountain? What if you could …"

She was confused. He said he had come to see her, but now he was talking about … *what was he talking about?*

He saw her confused look.

"I'm wondering if you would ever consider leaving this to work on bigger projects."

She drew back. Why would he ask this?

"I can't, Johnny." She was close to tears and found it hard to talk with the lump in her throat. She felt as though something heavy had been dropped on her chest. "I thought you knew that. Understood that."

He drew back too and seemed to be reconsidering his thoughts.

"I'm not saying this right." He took a deep breath. "Everything that's happened this summer has changed me. I'm not going to be farming anymore. That's why Paul and Naomi are on the farm."

This stunned her.

"You love your farm."

"I know, I know. But there's something else I have to do. I've taken a job with Bill McCollum's mission network. I'll be farming, in a sense. Planting. Nurturing. And I thought—"

He stopped, searching for words. He seemed to have gotten himself in a tangle.

She waited.

"I would very much like it if we could do it together."

She frowned.

"Do it together? We'd be doing ... what?"

"No, I mean ... We'd build our life together—" She felt a thrill at those words—"around mission projects. I'd be working with Bill's projects. You could be building orphanages."

She stared at him. Johnny—glib-tongued Johnny, who could talk himself into or out of anything—couldn't find the words to tell her he wanted to marry her.

But knowing he wanted to marry her did not move the heavy thing off her chest. She could not leave here. Not even to be Johnny's wife. God had put her here. He had given her a mission. How could she set that aside or trade it away for ... *a husband?*

But here was Johnny, wanting her to be with him. Finally telling her—in his own way—that he loved her. Coming all this way to find her. Johnny. Dear Johnny. *But, oh Lord, why is it happening in this way? Do I really have to choose between him and You?*

Johnny was watching her closely. She felt sick.

"Mariposa! Mariposa!"

Disregarding all respect for Audrey's privacy, two of the children came bursting around the bushes, their faces alight and their voices shrill with excitement as they repeated the Spanish word for *butterfly.*

"The butterflies are coming!"

"The Monarchs are back!"

Audrey rose from her chair and Johnny from his rock. Before they could follow the children out into the yard and road, something like an orange banner filled the turquoise sky above them. A strange, soft beating—like the beating of a heart—was moving through the village with the cloud of butterflies.

Wide-eyed, Johnny gazed upward, his mouth open.

"I've never imagined anything like this," he said. "There must be millions of them."

A few dozen of the tired travelers drifted downward, as though knowing they would find rest in Audrey's sanctuary. Three stopped at the bird bath, their frail wings slowing and folding as they drank. Some fluttered around the shriveled plants. The children danced among them, like a dance through snowflakes, their arms in the air, reaching up to the Monarchs.

One Monarch landed on Johnny's arm, a brilliant patch of orange against the pale blue fabric. He lifted his arm slowly, carefully, to look closely at the butterfly.

"Amazing," he said softly. "Annie loved these butterflies. If only she could have seen this! I wonder if she's seen anything like this in Heaven."

He was still in love with Annie.

39

Audrey did not sleep much that night.

They had given Johnny a bunk in the room with the older boys, and every now and then she could hear their voices and laughter. Johnny and the boys couldn't speak each other's language, but somehow they seemed to be having a good time together. At supper, Johnny had charmed the children, and they chattered away to him in Spanish. He would nod and laugh and make faces and gestures as though he understood it all, and they loved it.

He was here. He said he had come to see her. She was sure he wanted to ask her to marry him, but he also seemed to be asking her to leave this place. How could he?

She asked the question a hundred times that night: *Lord, why is it happening this way? What are You doing?*

From the day they had met, she had felt a special connection to Johnny. She had often laughed at stories of someone saying after first meeting a person, "I just met the man I'm going to marry." She had never believed such things—until it had happened to her. From that first day they had spent together in California, up at the horse farm, she had felt that Johnny was the only man she could ever possibly consider as a husband. Through her father's lost wallet, God had seen to it that their paths had crossed.

But there seemed to be so many obstacles! Chief among the hindrances to their romance was the fact that he was Amish and she was not.

At this thought, she sat up in bed and spoke, directing her words toward the boys' room.

"Are you still Amish? What are you thinking?" she said aloud.

Then, with a sigh, she let her body fall back against her pillow.

She tried praying. She banged her fists on God's door throughout the night. But there was no answer.

And there was no rest.

***

At breakfast, Johnny looked cheerful and refreshed, and the children renewed their adoration of their guest. Audrey was quiet, almost angry with him.

She felt his eyes on her, but she couldn't meet his gaze, and she knew that the children also sensed there was something amiss. The little one she had held, trembling in her arms the day before, came to her after breakfast and climbed into her lap, trying his best to get his small arms around her. The lump in her throat began growing again.

Johnny came to her then and reached out a hand.

"Let's take a walk," he said.

"There's nowhere, really, to walk, except down the road," replied Audrey. "There are trails up through the mountains, but I've never gone far."

"Then we'll take a short walk," said Johnny. Still holding her hand, he led her around the back of the building, back to her sanctuary.

She did not want to be there now.

He pulled her chair even closer to his rock and made a grand gesture for her to sit. Then he sat down on the rock in front of her.

"Yesterday didn't turn out quite like I planned," he began. His blue eyes held hers. She could not look away. "I have so much to tell you, that it all just came pouring out, and it came in all the wrong way and at the wrong time.

"Plus," he gave her one of those grins that made her feel as if she was the only person in the world and nothing could break the bond between them, "when I'm sitting right in front of you, I can't always think straight."

She closed her eyes for just a moment, wondering if she could believe what she saw on his face. He took her hands in his and gave them a squeeze. "Let's start again," he said gently.

She opened her eyes and he withdrew his hands and fished in his pants pocket, taking out a folded piece of notebook paper.

"I'm sorry. I couldn't find anything fancier. One of the boys gave me this last night. And no one had an envelope," he said. "Here."

He put the folded piece of paper in her hand and his fingers cupped around hers, as though he were handing her his dearest treasure.

"What? What is it?" Audrey asked.

"Please read it."

"Now?"

"Now." He released her hands and sat back, watching her.

She unfolded the single sheet and read.

Dear Audrey,

I saw the look on your face earlier tonight, and I realized I've done it all wrong.

In the Amish church, in trying to care for widows and orphans, it's customary for preachers or bishops to arrange marriages of widows and widowers. My dad had several letters written to him, inquiring if I might be interested in meeting widows. I know it's not the way most people would try to find a husband or wife, but it has worked in many instances in Amish communities.

(I am realizing that, even though I might be leaving the Amish church, there is much of that life that I do not want to relinquish.)

So, last night, when—in spite of all my planning—things didn't seem to be going too well, I wondered how to properly do what I came to do. I decided to write just such a letter. Except, in this instance, this is a widower, pleading his own case for consideration.

Much has changed with me. I am no longer part of the Amish church because Jesus has called me to do something that an Amish man cannot do. This has nothing to do with faith or belief, but with church rules and traditions. As I told my mom and dad, I did not choose to leave the Amish; I chose to follow Jesus.

I have come to believe that God has been leading me to this path all along. Ever since I decided to let Jesus guide me through life, He has been guiding, even though I didn't realize it. Every step of the way—in my marriage to and loss of Annie, my bike ride and the people I met along the way, my accident—in everything, God has been working.

You, Audrey, are a part of that plan God has for me. I believe it with all my heart. Not only did God plan to give me a companion in life who can help me on this path, but he changed my heart so that my heart could fall in love—something I thought would never happen again after I lost Annie.

Audrey looked up at Johnny, her eyes full, the tears ready to spill over. He was looking at her somberly, with a face full of love.

She went back to reading, but the words were blurry through her tears.

We had some obstacles along the way. For whatever reason, God's timing seemed difficult for us. But He works in all things for those who love Him.

So, even though we again seem to be at different places—different countries, even—I believe with all my heart that God is still working in both our lives and in the mission He's given to both of us.

From this point forward, I would like us to follow Jesus together. I don't know how we'll work out your mission here and my responsibilities in many other countries. But if God can change my heart and give me a new life, He can certainly work out the details of the new life He's given me.

I just thought of this as I wrote that last sentence!—Bill did tell me that I can live anywhere in the world!

However, if we live here, dear Audrey, I want to build you a house of our own. And you will have an electric iron.

Audrey looked up at Johnny again. The tears were now streaming down her cheeks and falling onto her shirt. She drew in a gulping breath and tried to get her words out.

"Yes. *Yes!*"

EPILOGUE

October 2017

Johnny had climbed the steps and sat down at the base of the cross, exactly as he remembered doing so many decades ago in Texas. The children, tiring of their game, plopped down next to him.

"Why did you make it so big, Grandpa?" asked the youngest of the three.

"Because it's so important," quipped the oldest, sounding wise. Johnny smiled at her.

"Yes, because it's so important. And because I want it to draw people to come and see it. You know, when I was your age, there were no tourists here. Now people come from everywhere to see Amish Country. They think there's an attraction here that compels them to come." His eyes went to the county road below. In his boyhood, two or three cars might pass the farm in an entire day. Now, the traffic was constant.

"Visitors like the food, the crafts, the peace, and the serenity here, but most of the time, they go back home and don't really know the real reason this area is so special. This is a blessed community because our parents and grandparents and their parents honored God. Then blessings get handed down from generation to generation. But that heritage only gets passed on if we honor God ourselves and don't take it for granted.

"I want folks who are driving along out on the highway to see this cross looming out of the darkness, and I want them to be curious enough to come here. I want them to know that the cross promises a new life. When they come, many read these Bible verses on the stones, and they learn some of the same things I learned long ago in Texas.

"It's not the cross that changes people. The cross is empty."

"That's because Jesus isn't dead anymore!" inserted the middle grandchild, who had grown an inch when his grandfather handed him the buggy reins. Johnny grinned at him.

"Yes, that's right. And it's what Jesus did when He died on the cross that will change lives. Many people come here who don't know Jesus, but they can find out about Him here, free of charge. It could be the most important day of their lives."

He looked up again at the empty cross, and the children could tell that He was drifting away from them, into memories again.

Down at the home place, a familiar figure walked out to the barn and lifted an arm to catch the rope on the bell that hung there. Johnny remembered how that bell had rung the day Annie died. Now, it was simply ringing to call them to lunch.

"All right children, it sounds like Grandma Audrey and Aunt Naomi have lunch ready. I'm hungry! Let's go!"

POSTSCRIPT

Those of you who have known Johnny since he had his first taste of beer at the age of 10 might be wondering what has happened to some of the people who have left their footprints in his life. Here's an update.

Wandering Willie. Willie was attacked one night while he was sleeping on the beach. He was beaten and robbed, and he died before anyone found him. When his body was discovered, it was thought he was a vagabond, until a resident who had known him told authorities that he used to be a prominent citizen. An investigation found that he had expired leaving 10 million dollars in a bank account. He had never named a beneficiary and no relatives claimed him—that is, not until news of the money was released. Then multiple close friends and family members came forward. None of the claims held up, and the State of California declared itself the recipient of the small fortune, dispersed it to liberal causes, and saw it squandered in less than an hour.

Joe Byler. Joe became an ordained Mennonite minister in Indiana. He spent one weekend a month in Chicago's inner city, volunteering at a homeless shelter.

Christine (Graber) Troyer. After Joe relinquished any claim on Christine, she was adopted by Paul and Naomi and came to live on the Miller farm by the end of that summer. As she grew up and before she joined the Amish Church, she flew with Johnny and Audrey on several mission trips abroad. She is now married to

Mark, a furniture builder who is also a preacher in the New Order Amish Church. They have four children and live in Mervin and Lizzie Klein's place on the other side of Strawberry Hill. The Klein farm no longer exists, though. Christine and Mark have five acres with a barn and pasture for their horse and a large garden, but a previous owner sold off the rest of the farmland and it has been developed into a retirement condo community.

Paul and Naomi. After adopting Christine, Paul and Naomi had an additional five children. They farmed the Miller farm until Simon was old enough to take over.

John and Mandy. Johnny's parents lived into their upper eighties. They passed away within one week of each other, and are awaiting the return of Jesus beside Annie up in the cemetery on Strawberry Hill.

Johnny and Audrey. Johnny and Audrey were married in Laredo, Texas. It was quite an occasion. Never had Johnny seen such a gathering of diverse people as at their wedding. Audrey, of course, looked stunning she walked down the aisle with her father, Samuel Cohraine. This was also the first time Johnny met Audrey's sister, Dawn. George and Millie were there, too, camping in the church parking lot with their house on wheels. Through the entire day of celebration, Millie beamed and cried and held hands with her George.

Johnny and Audrey were frequent guests back at his house on the Miller farm. That house still remains available for their use to this day.

They spent the next 40 years in missions. Johnny became an authority on setting up agricultural plots to feed many areas, and together they founded 10 orphanages in foreign countries.

Three children blessed their lives, two boys and one girl. The three often joined their parents on mission trips to foreign lands.

The oldest son, David, became a doctor. He and his wife, Lydia, became the first doctor-teacher couple in the village in Mexico where Audrey had taught. The orphanage no longer exists, but in the forest high up on the mountain behind the village there is now the Monarch Butterfly Biosphere Reserve, where millions of Monarch butterflies winter each year and visitors can witness trees layered in orange and black, one of the amazingly intricate details of God's creation.

The Millers' second child was a daughter named Anna Elizabeth. (Johnny questioned why Audrey would want her daughter carrying the same name as his first wife. However, Audrey was so confidant in herself that she knew what she wanted and never looked back.) Johnny admitted he was a bit biased since Anna Elizabeth was his daughter, but he believed she was, without a doubt, the most beautiful lady (next to Audrey, of course) he had ever seen. Anna Elizabeth was a bit headstrong, which Johnny kiddingly said came from the Cohraine genes. Of course, he knew better. She had Audrey's looks, but she was as ornery as Johnny ever had been. Anna Elizabeth admired her father and would often tag along with her dad to all corners of the globe. Therefore, it surprised no one who knew her that when Johnny retired from his position with Big Bill's mission projects, it was Anna Elizabeth Miller who replaced her father. Many men tried but all failed to woo her. She was focused like a laser beam, intent on changing the world. She was in love with a man, a man called Jesus. (But she's still single, so there's still a chance.)

John Miller III completed the family. He had so many nicknames, no one could keep track of them all. In reality and the Amish tradition, he was John's Johnny's John. "Triple J" some called him. Some just used "JR." He preferred "John," and later in life, after working up through the ranks, he carried business cards that read *John J. Miller. President, McCollum Equipment Company.*

Sydney. You will remember that Johnny met this fellow at a commune in California. He was the designer and tailor who made the Johnny Barndoor pants. Sydney kept his end of the bargain and sent royalty checks to Johnny for several years. It was quite a return on investment for Johnny's $20.

Johnny never saw Sydney again. After a few years, though, he wrote a letter to Sydney and asked him to no longer send any money. It just didn't seem right. Johnny requested, instead, that his share of the profits would be donated to a food bank.

Bill McCollum. While Johnny was abroad, he received the unexpected news that Big Bill had passed away. He rushed home in time for the funeral and had the honor of being a pallbearer for this great man who had helped change so many lives, especially his.

Following the funeral, Bill's wife, Penny, asked to speak to Johnny. She told him that Bill's passing was the calmest passing from one world to the next she had ever seen. (She volunteered at a local hospice, so she had seen many.) Bill had seemed so excited to see what was on the other side!

"Here, he wrote a note to you," she said. "And he asked me to give you these." She reached into her purse and dropped a set of keys into Johnny's hand. "Those are the keys to that old pickup he drove. He said you would know what to do with it."

Johnny opened the note and could almost hear Bill's booming voice as he read. *Park this truck up by that cross you had built, and when folks ask why that old relic is there, tell them our story.*

The Cross. Tourism became a lucrative business in Johnny's home community. Even the Amish built very successful businesses on it.

When Johnny made the decision to erect the cross on Strawberry Hill, he had a list of Amish millionaires and other successful Christian businessmen who he hoped would contribute funds. The entire three million was raised before he got to the end of his list.

The cross was dedicated one beautiful autumn evening. It was the event of the decade. Folks came from everywhere. Politicians of every stripe appeared, including the governor of Ohio.

Some were there to witness the folly of wasting so much money. Yes, of course there were detractors. There always are when someone has a dream. Especially so when one invades the devil's territory. Most of the detractors were silenced that evening when the lights were turned on and the brilliance of the illuminated cross shone across the valley.

The planning of the program for the evening had somehow gotten out of hand. Johnny wasn't comfortable with the lineup of speakers. There was too much talk about the economic impact this "attraction" could have on the community. That interested Johnny not one bit. The cross wasn't there for economic reasons. It created no jobs. He would never charge an admission. However, it *would* change lives. He was certain of that.

Big Bill gave a prayer of dedication. His prayer rang out over the surrounding countryside.

Johnny was the last speaker for the evening. As he got up to speak, he broke down and wept. He could not speak one word. Audrey came to his rescue. She stood and took a few steps to stand beside him, taking the notes he had jotted down. She glanced at them, and then shoved them into her pocket.

Pointing across the road, she began.

"Over in that cemetery is a great lady. We are all here tonight because of her, Annie Miller. One person. An Amish person, at that. The choices Annie made in life brought us all here together tonight. One person can make a difference in many lives."

Turning back toward the cross, Audrey pointed skyward.

"Because of one Person's choice to accept death on the cross, we can also have our lives transformed and have the assurance we will someday join those departed ones in Heaven.

"And for every one of us, one choice makes the difference between life and death, between the chains of our old life or the joy of a new life. The cross makes all the difference."

Mike. Although Johnny never saw Mike again, there were some rumors floating about the countryside that neighbors sometimes thought they had seen the silver-haired driver up at the cross. When memories of that trip to Indiana crossed Johnny's mind, he would often muse about the familiarity he had felt when he met Mike—the man had reminded him of someone, but he could never say exactly *who*. Finally, on a hot, steamy day while Johnny was being transported up the Amazon River in a canoe, he watched the swirl of water and remembered the man he had pulled from the Mississippi River. That was it! Mike and River Man. So much alike, they could have been brothers.

Samuel Cohraine. Although Johnny's father-in-law never became what could be described as a Christian dynamo, his life was changed. He quit the marriage-dissolving business and spent more time out on his horse farm. He also did counseling with couples who were experiencing marriage problems, inviting them up to the farm, where they could work out resolutions in a relaxed environment. Samuel did, after all, have a wealth of knowledge about what tore marriages apart, so it was his hope that he could intervene in such situations before it was too late. He was accurate in that perception and was quite successful in his endeavor.

Simon. Johnny's nephew Simon was an anomaly. Most people imagined he would end up living the traditional Amish lifestyle. They were wrong. Simon was a protégé of Johnny, virtually a clone, if you will. As a youngster, he was a good worker when one could pry him from the tree house. He was greatly influenced by the notes Johnny had written and left there. Simon felt a bit of an intruder when reading them, but he found them so helpful in answering his own questions about spirituality.

As a teenager, Simon jumped at the chance to travel overseas with his uncle. Family members were convinced the lure of adventure would also take Simon from the farm. They were wrong. Simon discovered a heart for missions while abroad. However, his concern was for the mission field right back home, in the heart of Amish Country. He returned home, joined the church, got engaged (or *called out*, as they say in the Amish church), and was married. He began farming with Paul and developed an intense desire for Bible reading.

In time, the church needed to ordain another minister. Simon's grandfather was ill and could no longer be counted on to preach. The ordination service would be held at the Miller home place, and the night before the service, the Holy Spirit revealed to Simon that he would be chosen.

Now, being ordained as an Amish minister is not something greatly desired by most men. It's also quite a task to be a preacher's wife, and their children are often watched closely by other church members. These men have no formal training. They are chosen by lot, and the lot is trusted to be God's designation of who should next be in leadership. In most cases, the chosen man does an admirable job. When one reads and studies the Bible and allows the Holy Spirit to rule, amazing things happen with common folks. Maybe it is precisely the lack of training that enables these men to live in utter dependence on God for wisdom.

Simon actually was fine with the word that he would be chosen. He knew more changes were coming, and he wanted to be involved in those changes. The next morning, he told his bride that she was going to be married to a minister before the day was done.

During the service, church members file through a side room and whisper the name of the person they think should be chosen. Then the men with a certain amount of mentions are summoned to the front bench, where the bishop has placed the same number of songbooks as men. A piece of paper with a Bible verse has been inserted in one book. The bishop shuffles the books and lays them out on a table. One by one, the candidates rise to pick up a book. Simon immediately knew the lot was in the center book. For a moment, he considered waiting and letting the other men pick the book from either side, kind of a "putting out a fleece," he thought. The man beside him was sweating profusely. There were a few things in his life that would need to go if he was picked, and he really didn't want to let go of them. Simon reconsidered his own situation, then rose to his feet and grasped the middle book. He knew he was meant to do it.

A gasp went through the crowd when it was revealed that Simon was the chosen one. He would be the youngest ever to be ordained in that district church.

Jesus' command to preach the gospel and make disciples everywhere drove Simon's life. He preached boldly about the blood of Jesus cleansing from all sin and the new life that comes to those who believe in Jesus. He had numerous conversations with other Amish folks about being more open about what they believed and why they were Amish. With the millions of tourists passing through their area, they had a field ripe for harvest. Oh, Simon got opposition. He was gathering forces to make incursions into the devil's territory.

Slowly a spiritual breeze drifted through the Amish community. It wasn't just Simon. There were other ministers—young and old—with a yearning for more spirituality. They believed both tradition and spirituality could coexist.

Simon also met with groups of Amish business owners and employees. He would talk about how to answer questions from outsiders as the Amish met the world—queries such as those about the head coverings, the plain dress, and the avoidance of many things the world thinks are necessities were opportunities, he said. "We have an opportunity to plant some seeds in a person's life," was his oft-repeated line. (Some people, sometimes in mockery, sometimes in respect, referred to him as Seed Simon.)

There were days when the Holy Spirit prompted Simon to walk up to Strawberry Hill. Invariably, someone showed up at the cross that day and Simon talked with them. God set up the meetings.

After Johnny retired, he and Audrey were more often at the farm, and Simon and Johnny spent many evenings in discussions of Scripture—discussions that would likely stretch into the night.

Doug. Oh, yes, Dougie. I almost forgot about him. The last we heard about him was that he was a prisoner of war somewhere in the jungles of Viet Nam. The story about his rescue and return home is simply amazing. An entire book could be written about that rescue. Maureen, Doug's mom, had been correct—Johnny was the person God had sent to set everything in motion. Of course, Johnny didn't go to Viet Nam, but he was the one who called Big Bill, and Big Bill pulled strings to make it all happen, and the whole thing was nothing short of a miracle.

I considered writing about that daring rescue (someday), but I promised my editor there would be no more fiction books. So my hands are tied. I tried, I really tried, but they are tied.

A Note from the Author

In many ways, writing a book is similar to building a house.

A house needs a strong foundation whereon can be constructed a good, solid structure. Any good book requires the foundation of a strong story line, around which the characters can be built.

A finished home does not display the many necessities of infrastructure. Behind beautiful finished walls are networks of wires, pipes, insulation, and other essentials that frame and complete the building. Also invisible is the infrastructure of a finished book—the editing, proofreading, layout and cover design, and printing processes.

Too often, the author gets the credit for the finished product, and many people who have also spent hours producing the book go unnoticed and at times unappreciated.

The employees at Carlisle Printing have been tireless in their efforts to produce quality products for Wandering Home Books. Thank you. I appreciate your skills and diligence.

A special debt of gratitude is owed to my editor, Elaine Starner, for once again collaborating with me on another construction project. Being the author equates me to the general contractor of a project. That would make Elaine the job foreman. Or, more aptly, job forewoman. Elaine and I will soon be working on our ninth project together.

I'm often asked what my next project will be. In November of 2016, I hiked throughout Israel with a friend. Backpacking and hitchhiking, we followed a trail known as the Jesus Trail, starting in Nazareth and ending at Capernaum, by the Sea of Galilee. We extended our hike to include the Golan Heights and the city of Jerusalem.

My purpose on this hike was to further my understanding of what it really means to live a Christian life. What does "believing in Jesus" really mean? I'm aware many well-intentioned folks believe facts *about* Jesus—but just believing about Jesus is not enough. Most Muslims and many non-Christians believe about Jesus. Believing *in* Him, I'm convinced, is a different matter.

And then, does believing in Jesus require anything more of us? If so, what does it require? When He says to us today, "Follow me," what is He asking of us?

My goal and desire in my next book is to help fellow pilgrims determine what it means in their own lives to believe in Jesus and follow Him.

This book, based on my hike in Israel, will be released in November of 2017. It is tentatively titled *The 13th Disciple.* As I walked through some of the same landscapes where Jesus walked, I imagined myself back in time, following Jesus as the thirteenth disciple. (I did not quite make the cut for the original twelve.)

As we move on to Israel, we say goodbye to Johnny Miller. I am often asked if I am the character of Johnny in *The Wanderers* series. I usually just grin and deny everything. For the sake of full disclosure now, I'll admit it—I'm not Johnny. (Or, Johnny's not me.) However, all of my characters are based on composites of people I know or have known. I've used characteristics and traits of friends and relatives, to be sure.

God has blessed me with a vivid imagination and with precious memories of a wonderful past. *The Wanderers* series was my attempt to relive many of those memories.

The setting for this series of novels is my grandmother's farm in Walnut Creek, Ohio. As a youth, I spent many glorious weeks there during the summers. My sisters and cousins did the same.

There actually was a wash house on the farm, and it, too, was dismantled—it just never transformed into a tree house.

Walnut Creek turned into Johnny's Milford. Charm, Ohio, became Pine Grove. The county seat of Holmes County is Millersburg, and I named that town Stevenson. There's even a small airport in Millersburg, should you wish to fly in to visit our area.

If you ever do come to Amish Country, stop up and visit me on Strawberry Hill.

Paul Stutzman

Made in United States
North Haven, CT
17 December 2021

12994707R00134